Dan

Dune House Cozy Mystery Series

Cindy Bell

Copyright © 2017 Cindy Bell

All rights reserved.

This is a work of fiction. The characters, incidents and locations portrayed in this book and the names herein are fictitious. Any similarity to or identification with the locations, names, characters or history of any person, product or entity is entirely coincidental and unintentional.

All trademarks and brands referred to in this book are for illustrative purposes only, are the property of their respective owners and not affiliated with this publication in any way. Any trademarks are being used without permission, and the publication of the trademark is not authorized by, associated with or sponsored by the trademark owner.

ISBN-13: 978-1543059809

ISBN-10: 1543059805

Table of Contents

Chapter One

Salt laced the air as it drifted beneath her nostrils. Mary drew in a lung-filling breath, then released it in a slow sigh. At times she still had to remind herself that this wasn't a dream. She really was living right by the sea, in a grand house that she and her best friend, Suzie, had renovated into its former glory as a bed and breakfast. She'd transitioned from the tail-end of a rough marriage and a rougher divorce, into what she could only describe as paradise.

"More cream?" Suzie nudged a small cornflower blue pitcher towards her.

"Yes, thank you." Mary picked up the pitcher and poured a bit more cream into her lukewarm coffee. They'd been sitting on the porch that overlooked the water since dawn. Now that the little town of Garber was coming alive, Mary glanced at her watch. "I can't believe that in a few more hours Cathy and Ben will be here."

"I'm so excited to see them." Suzie picked up her mug of coffee and took a tiny sip. "I'm sure they'll both have so much to tell you."

"They've been so busy lately, I've barely heard from them." Mary gazed out across the water as it rippled with lazy waves. "I've never felt so distant from them before."

"It's only natural." Suzie placed her hand over Mary's and offered a gentle squeeze. "They are busy right now, but soon they will be calling you night and day for advice."

"You're right." Mary tipped her head towards a small shack further down the beach. "It looks like Curtis is already at it this morning. I can see a light on in the shack."

"He grabbed a cup of coffee on his way out this morning. He said the weather was perfect for a long dive."

"It's so nice to have him nearby. I've learned

so much about diving since he's been here," Mary said.

"Me too. Although, I'm not sure that I'm ready to take the plunge myself."

"Me neither." Mary laughed. "I think I'm better off on dry land. However, I bet Ben and Cathy would love it."

"Oh, what a great idea! I know Trish and Hal have been taking lessons from him since they've been here. They said it was one of the highlights of their romantic getaway at Dune House. Trish told me he's a fantastic teacher."

"I'm sure he is." Mary cleared her throat and took the last swallow of her coffee.

"Wait a minute, what's that about?" Suzie met her eyes across the table.

"Hm? Nothing."

"Oh no, that wasn't nothing. That was something."

"No, not really. Trish and Hal are nice kids."

"They're in their thirties, only about twenty years younger than us."

"Still kids." Mary smiled and picked up Suzie's empty mug. "Time to get things straightened up, and breakfast ready for Trish and Hal. Do you want me to toast you a bagel?"

"Sure, thank you. I'll check the linens and run the vacuum upstairs after Trish and Hal are up." Suzie paused at the door. "Oops, I forgot we can't go in or out this way. When did that locksmith say he was coming?"

"He is supposed to be here today, but I'm not holding my breath. I've heard he's not the most reliable guy, but he's the only one in town, and you said you want to use only local businesses wherever possible."

"I know, it's worth the wait to put our money into our local economy. If he's not here by tomorrow, we'll have to get someone else though. I'm too old and tired to be walking all the way around to the front."

"Ha! You're old and tired?" Mary rolled her eyes. "Tell me another one."

As they walked around to the front of Dune House Suzie caught a glimpse of the shack on the beach again.

"I hope his business does well. I'd love to see him stay here."

"Me too. He seems like a nice person." Mary opened the door and held it open for Suzie.

"He'll attract a younger crowd, too." Just as Suzie stepped into Dune House her cell phone chimed. She picked it up to see that she had a text message.

"Oh, it's from Jason! He's letting us know that he and Summer landed just fine and are having a great time."

"Wonderful!" Mary smiled. "I'm so glad to hear it."

"Me too. I hope they really have a chance to relax and enjoy married life. They had to wait so long before they could go away on their honeymoon."

"Yes, they did, I'm sure they're treasuring every moment."

Mary thought about Wes being away for a family wedding and wished he was there. He had asked her to come along, but with her children visiting she had declined. She surprised herself when she missed him as they hadn't been going out for very long, but this was the first time that they had been apart from each other for more than a few days.

Mary lingered in the kitchen to prepare breakfast for their guests, while Suzie went to the laundry room to collect the linens she'd washed the night before. It wasn't always easy to keep up with all of the needs of Dune House, but she loved every minute. There was nowhere else on Earth she would rather be. Of course that was because of more than just the rambling three story home she'd inherited from an estranged uncle. It was her cousin Jason, Mary, and all of the people she'd met in Garber that made her so content. After many years of believing she never wanted to settle down, she discovered that she had finally found the place where she belonged. As she opened the door to the laundry room she heard voices. They sounded strange, as if they were floating from thin air. After a moment she realized that they were coming through the laundry chute from the third floor.

"You're being ridiculous, Hal. You're seeing things that aren't there."

"Am I?" His voice was stern. "Because every time I turned around you were smiling at him, touching him, or laughing at one of his stupid jokes."

"They're not stupid, they're funny, that's why I'm laughing. Of course I'm going to be friendly, he's teaching us how to dive."

"Just watch how friendly you get." The voice drifted away as the couple walked further away from the laundry chute. Suzie cringed. She tried not to get too involved in private matters, especially those of her guests, but it sounded like quite a bit of tension brewed between the couple. She finished gathering the linens then left the laundry room.

Suzie could hear Hal and Trish as they talked with Mary around the dining room table. Everything sounded calmer. She tried not to focus on the argument. As far as she knew it was normal for married couples to squabble. That was one of the main reasons she never wanted to get married. She hated the idea of having to answer for her every move and thought. No matter how many times other people told her that marriage wasn't always that way, she didn't want to risk it. Still, for some reason the pesky desire to get hitched had crept up lately and she was having a hard time ignoring it. She blamed it on Paul, a fisherman who had sailed into her life, and taken her heart by storm. At least, that was the way she remembered it. As much as she tried to fight it, she enjoyed spending time with him, and even missed him when he was out on the water. Luckily, she had the bed and breakfast to distract her.

As Suzie vacuumed the upstairs she hummed to herself. She'd never expected to be content in domestic activities, but when it came to her role as caretaker she took it very seriously. As she vacuumed near the window she noticed a taxi pull up. Excitement raced through her as she realized that Mary's children had arrived. "Mary! Mary, they're here!" Suzie nearly tripped over the cord of the vacuum as she ran down the hallway. She caught herself on the wall and straightened up as she reached the stairs. Mary passed the bottom of the stairs as she hurried towards the front door, though her troublesome knees caused her to move a bit slower than she would like. Suzie managed to catch up with her at the door.

"Okay, wait a minute." She caught Mary's hand before she could open the door. "Deep breath, right?"

"Yes, deep breath." Mary took a long, deep breath and held it for a moment before she released it again. Then she opened the door. She found her daughter Cathy on the other side.

"Mom!" Cathy flung her arms wide open. It was as touching to Mary to see her adult daughter seek her embrace as it had been the first time Cathy had reached for her as a baby. She wrapped her arms around her and mumbled into her long auburn hair. "I promised myself I wasn't going to cry."

"No, no crying." Cathy looked into her eyes. "This is a happy moment, right?"

"Yes, you're right." Mary blinked back the tears that had already formed. "I'm so glad to see you, Cathy. You look as beautiful as ever."

"Aw, thanks Mom. This is Rick." Cathy gestured to a young man that hauled two suitcases up the wide, wooden front steps of the porch.

"Oh." Mary blinked. "Nice to meet you, Rick." She looked back at her daughter with wide eyes.

"Didn't you get my text?" Cathy frowned.

"No. What did it say?"

"That I was bringing my boyfriend Rick along with me." She grimaced. "I hope that's okay."

"Oh sure, of course it is. Rick, you must be a very special person if my daughter is fond of you."

"Thanks." He grinned and thrust out his hand. "It's nice to meet you, too."

"You should have seen these two in the taxi on the way here." Ben rolled his brown eyes and heaved a soft zippered bag up on to his shoulder as he climbed the steps. "Ugh, please, don't leave me alone with them again."

"Aw, Ben, don't give your sister a hard time. Your time will come," Mary said as she gave him a big hug.

"Listen to Mom, soon enough it'll be you with a girl on your arm. Oh, I don't know, maybe when you're sixty?"

"Keep quiet, Catherine!" Ben exclaimed.

"Cathy, be nice to your brother."

"I was being nice, he's the one who..."

"Hello? Is anyone going to hug Aunt Suzie?" Suzie grinned and opened her arms to both of them. The argument was forgotten as Cathy and Ben each took a turn hugging Suzie. Suzie savored the embraces. The only time she doubted her choice not to have children was when Cathy and Ben were around. She loved them almost as much as she imagined she would love her own. The benefit was that she never had to change a diaper, and when they had a problem that was over her head, she could just send them to Mary. "How was your flight?"

"It was fine. A little bumpy." Ben shrugged. "For a second there I thought Cathy was going to try to jump out."

"I was a little nervous." She laughed. "Luckily

Rick was there to calm me down."

"I'm glad you're all here safe. I can show you your rooms." Mary smiled as she led them towards the hall.

"I'll get the bags," Suzie said.

"Oh no, it's fine, I can get them." Rick tightened his grip on the handles. "They're pretty heavy."

"Don't worry, I can handle it." Suzie was so used to helping guests with their bags that the offer was automatic.

"It's all right, I'll get them." He cleared his throat. "It wouldn't feel right to me to let you carry my bags. It wouldn't be respectful."

"Ah, a rare gentleman?"

"Some say that, yes." He smiled, a charming smile, that made Suzie stare at him a little harder. She was always a little suspicious of anyone who was too polite. Like they were trying too hard.

"Feel free, I appreciate the help." Suzie smiled

as he walked past her and followed Mary down the hallway.

"I'm afraid I wasn't expecting you to have a guest, Cathy, so I only have two rooms made up, and I guess, well."

"Mom, don't worry. Rick can bunk with Ben. Right Ben?"

"Seriously?" Ben sighed. "I guess so."

"Just until I get another room made up, sweetheart."

"We'll have some time to bond, it'll be great, Ben." Rick ruffled his hair.

"Great." Ben rolled his eyes, but opened the door to his room and let Rick follow after him. While they settled in their rooms, Mary joined Suzie in the kitchen.

"I figured I'd get some snacks together for them, they're probably hungry after the flight."

"Good idea, Suzie. I just can't believe that they're here. I'm so excited."

"The boyfriend was a surprise, hmm?"

"Yes, he was. But honestly I'm glad that he's here. I'd rather Cathy bring him to meet me than to have to wonder about who he is and what he's like. Now I'll have the chance to get to know him."

"That's a good point." Suzie smiled. "I'm glad that you're happy."

"What does that mean?"

"Huh?" She placed a plate of snacks on the dining room table.

"Suzie."

"What?" Her eyes widened.

"I know you, I know your tones, and that comment meant something. What is it?"

"Oh, I don't know. I just think maybe he's trying a little too hard."

"He's young and in love, if he wasn't trying hard, I'd be surprised."

"You're right. I think I'm just a little out of

touch with the younger generation."

"Don't you remember when we were the younger generation?" Mary grinned.

"Vaguely." Suzie laughed.

"I think I'll take these into the living room so we can all be comfortable." Mary picked up the tray.

"Go enjoy. I'll take care of lunch for the guests."

"Are you sure?"

"Absolutely." Suzie hugged her friend. "I'm so glad they're here. Now go spend as much time as you can with them."

"Thank you, I'll do just that." Mary carried the tray into the living room just as her two children and Rick emerged from the hallway. Rick and Cathy followed after her, but Ben paused in the kitchen beside Suzie.

"This place is even more amazing than the last time I visited. You've done so much more work on it. You did a great job with the upstairs."

"Thanks Ben." Suzie smiled at him. "You and your sister are welcome here anytime, you know that don't you?"

"Sure." He nodded and brushed his hair away from his eyes. He still reminded Suzie of a puppy dog, too cute for his own good. But he was getting older, and some of the little boy face had begun to fade. "I'm just glad Mom has this, you know. It's something to keep her occupied, and I know she loves it here."

"I'm glad she's here, too. I couldn't do it without her."

"How are her knees doing?"

"About the same."

"I'm worried about her."

"Try not to be, sweetie, she wouldn't want you to be. She's taking care of herself. I'd tell you if she wasn't."

"Okay good." He glanced over his shoulder

towards the living room. It seemed to Suzie that he didn't want to join in.

"Is everything okay, Ben? How is school going?"

"Not great." He frowned. "I'm having a hard time this year. It's so much harder than freshman year."

"Maybe some tutoring would help?"

"I'm in tutoring. It's like I just can't keep up. I'm working, and there's never any time for studying. I'm thinking of dropping out."

"Oh no, Ben, you can't do that."

"Why not?" He frowned. "Not everyone goes to college."

"No, that's true, but it's best if you do. It gives you a good foundation, even if you don't work in the field of your choice, you'll always have that degree to support whatever path you take."

"Now you sound like Mom, I thought you would be more understanding. I mean, I know you went to college, but your job wasn't exactly run of the mill, and what does investigative journalism have to do with running a bed and breakfast?"

"I worked as a journalist for years before I gave it up. I loved it. Then I discovered that I loved other things, too, and decided to expand my options. I do understand if you don't want a traditional career, and you know I'll support whatever you choose, but this is something you need to discuss with your mother. She has great advice to offer, and she knows you better than anyone else, maybe even better than yourself. You can trust her with this, Ben."

"What if she gets mad?" He sighed. "I've gotten myself into some problems lately. I've had to borrow money from my dad, and he's not happy about it."

"What's really going on, Ben?" She looked into his eyes. "Whatever it is, you can tell me."

"It's nothing. I just need to get my head on

straight. Thanks, Aunt Suzie."

"Ben, make sure you talk to your mother about this, all right? I promise, she's the most compassionate and understanding person I know. She only wants you to be happy."

"I will, I'll talk to her."

As Ben joined the others in the living room Suzie stared after him. Ben had always been the more sensitive of the two children. Suzie often thought he bore the brunt of his parents' failing relationship. Cathy seemed to understand and accept when things got hard, but Ben seemed angry and confused. She hoped he hadn't gotten himself into the kind of trouble that he couldn't get out of. Once lunch was prepared, Hal and Trish appeared long enough to fill their plates, then disappeared back to their room. Suzie thought it was a little odd, but knew that sometimes guests preferred to have privacy.

Chapter Two

After Suzie cleaned up from lunch she stepped out through the back door to check on a few things in the shed. Then she walked around the side of the house towards the front porch. It was a project that had been on her mind for a long time. She loved decorating and she'd been planning to stain some of the furniture and add some pieces that she and Mary picked up at estate sales. With the good weather she guessed it would be a good time to start on it. As she began to climb the stairs she was startled by a man seated in one of the rocking chairs on the porch. She didn't recognize him, and wasn't expecting any new guests to arrive. He stood up as she reached the top of the steps.

"Hi, I'm Jim." He thrust his hand towards her. She took it in a firm shake and looked into his eyes.

"I'm Suzie. We weren't expecting any guests.

Are you looking for a room?"

"Actually, I'm looking for a friend of mine. Curtis Malcolm. He's supposed to be staying here."

"Oh yes, Curtis is staying here. Right now he's out on a dive I think. You're welcome to come in and wait for him."

"No, that's all right. I'll stay out here if that's okay. I like the view."

"Well, it's even better on the other side." She smiled at him and pointed around the corner of the deck. "There are some lounge chairs out there. Feel free to relax and enjoy."

"Thanks so much." He tipped his hat to her then walked around the corner of the house. As she watched him go she noted that he was a fit man, perhaps in his late twenties. She was glad that Curtis had a friend visiting, as so far it didn't seem he'd made many connections with the locals, aside from perhaps Louis, the librarian.

When Suzie stepped back inside Dune House she began to get the items out she needed to prepare dinner for the guests. Mary usually did most of the cooking, but while her children were visiting Suzie wanted her to be as free as possible to enjoy them. She could hear some laughter from the living room and knew that they were already well into a good experience. It filled her heart with warmth to think that Mary was getting the reunion she had hoped for. Even though she was a fantastic mother, she knew that Mary still worried about whether the kids would hold the divorce against her, or with time forget how much she loved them. To Suzie, it seemed impossible, but she wasn't looking at it through a mother's eyes. As she finished preparing the vegetables for dinner she heard the sound of the back door of Dune House swing open, then close.

"I can't believe you came all of this way." She recognized Curtis' voice as it drifted through the entrance way.

"Why not? I can't let you have all of the fun," Jim replied. "It looks like you have a nice setup here."

"It is nice. I'm planning to rent a place in town, but nothing is available until the end of the month. So I've been staying here."

"Gorgeous house."

"Yes, it is. And the two ladies that run it are very kind."

"I noticed. So you'll have to take me down to your favorite dive spot around here."

"Sure, of course I will. Tomorrow maybe?"

"That sounds great. Do you mind if I crash here, too? It seems they might have some rooms available."

"Absolutely, I'll talk to Suzie about it for you. I'm sure she's got something open." As the pair walked into the kitchen Suzie turned away from the stove and smiled at them both.

"Curtis, I see you found your friend."

"Yes, I did, thanks for making him so comfortable. Jim needs a place to stay tonight. Do you have anything?"

"Just one night?" She met Jim's eyes.

"Maybe longer." Jim shrugged.

"Let's just start with one night. I'll even cover it for you, Jim. You can add it to my bill, Suzie."

"You don't need to do that, Curtis." Jim frowned. "I can cover my own."

"I insist. You've come all of this way just to see me. It's the least I could do."

"All right, thank you." Jim nodded.

"If you need to stay for longer, just let me know when you know." Suzie smiled. "I'll get a room ready for you right after dinner. You're welcome to join us."

"Thanks so much," Jim said.

"We'll be eating in about two hours."

"That's long enough for me to show you the

beach. You're not going to believe how clear the water is here." Curtis smiled.

"Great, let's go have a look."

"Oh Jim, do you have any luggage?" Suzie called out before the two men could reach the door.

"Just this bag." He pointed to the small bag on the floor. "I travel light."

"Anything you might need you can borrow from me. You know what's mine is yours." Curtis grinned.

"Sure, I know that." Jim nodded.

"You can leave it in my room if you want," Curtis offered.

"It's okay, I'll take it with me." Jim smiled. "It has my swimming stuff in it."

"I still have those ropes I borrowed from you."

The two disappeared through the front door. Suzie glanced at her watch. She now needed to get two rooms ready and make sure that dinner was on the table. She was just about to go to the linen closet when Mary stepped out of the living room and caught her arm.

"What are you up to?"

"I was going to make up a room for Ben, and our new guest."

"A new guest?"

"Yes, Jim, a friend of Curtis'."

"Well, just make up one, okay? I'd rather Ben stay with Rick. It'll keep things, well you know, separated."

"By things do you mean your adult daughter and her boyfriend?" Suzie raised an eyebrow.

"I just mean, things." Mary grimaced. "I might not be as modern as I like to think I am."

"Okay, no problem. I'm sure Ben won't mind. Have you had a chance to talk to him alone?"

"No, not really. Why? Is something wrong?"

"I just think that you should talk to him. Don't

tell him I said anything, but I think it's important."

"Okay, I will. Thanks for the heads up, Suzie."

"Always. Now get back in there and enjoy your kids."

"We're all going to go for a walk on the beach. I want them to soak up as much of this beauty as they can."

"Good idea."

"I'll be back in time to help with dinner."

"Don't you dare, I've got it. As far as I'm concerned, you're on vacation."

"Suzie, now we have almost a full house, you can't handle that alone."

"If I need you, I will let you know, I promise."

"All right." Mary hugged her, then joined the others as they walked towards the door. "I still haven't heard from the locksmith!"

"Okay, I'll see what I can do." Suzie opened

the door to the linen closet and pulled out some fresh sheets. Then she grabbed a basket of cleaning supplies and headed for one of the empty rooms. As a rule they cleaned a room after a guest left, but they also cleaned it before a guest checked in if it was vacant for more than a week, as on some occasions the rooms were empty long enough for dust to settle.

She made her way up to the third floor because it had the best views. It had three bedrooms and an additional bathroom. She opened the door to the first room and stepped inside. It hadn't been cleaned that long ago so the floors were still nice. She made the bed with fresh sheets and pillowcases. That was enough to work up a sweat. She opened the window to let some fresh air into the room. For a moment she paused and gazed out over the ocean. The green-blue surface stretched out so far that she grew dizzy at the sight of it. Somewhere out there, Paul was on his boat, maybe thinking about her. She smiled at the thought. When she spotted Curtis and Jim on the beach she was reminded that she had a lot to get done.

Suzie focused her attention on the rest of the room and made sure there wasn't a speck of dust left. Once she was sure that everything was ready she stepped out of the room and locked it behind her. When she reached the ground floor she headed straight to the kitchen and started preparing dinner. While Mary had a knack for cooking it took her quite a bit of concentration to keep things from boiling over or burning. As the kitchen began to fill with the aroma of the food she heard the sound of footsteps on the stairs. Hal and Trish reached the bottom and paused near the kitchen.

"Hi. How are you two doing? Do you need anything for the room?" Suzie asked.

"No, everything's fine." Hal frowned.

"Are you joining us for dinner?" Suzie smiled at Hal.

"No." He narrowed his eyes. "I think we'll

have dinner in town tonight."

"Oh why? It smells delicious!" Trish exclaimed.

"You know why. Let's go." He gripped her arm rather firmly and steered her away from the kitchen.

Suzie bit into her bottom lip as she heard the two biting back and forth at each other. As much as she didn't like to witness the fight, there was nothing that was too harsh said between them. She hoped that it stayed that way or improved.

Chapter Three

Suzie set the table with the dishes and silverware. Then she checked on the food in the oven again. As she closed the oven door, she heard the front door swing open and voices travel through the entrance.

"I'm telling you right now, there's money to be made in it. If you would consider investing, you and I could both be rich."

"I don't know, Jim. I'm not looking to make any big investments right now. I just got the dive shack opened up, and I haven't even turned a profit yet."

"But it'll be worth it." Jim clapped him on the shoulder as they walked into the dining room. "Just think about it, that's all I'm asking."

"All right, I will. Suzie, that smells amazing." Curtis grinned at her as he pulled out a chair. "I'm starving."

"Good, because there is plenty, and I expect you to have seconds at least."

"Seconds, guaranteed." Curtis chuckled.

"Me too!" Jim rubbed his stomach as he sat down beside Curtis.

The front door swung open again and Mary, along with her children, and Rick, stepped inside. While Mary introduced them to Curtis and Jim, Suzie brought the food out to the table. Soon they were all enjoying her attempt at pasta with a creamy chicken sauce.

"This is delicious, Suzie." Mary smiled.

"Thanks Mary." Suzie smiled back at her, though she doubted her friend was being completely honest about the taste. "Cathy, Ben, have you asked Curtis about diving lessons?"

"Oh, are you interested?" Curtis looked up as he swiped a piece of bread across his plate.

"Yes, absolutely." Cathy grinned.

"I'd like to check it out." Ben nodded.

"I'm already certified." Rick draped his arm along the back of Cathy's chair. "But I'd love for Cathy to learn so we can dive together."

"Great. We can get together for a lesson first thing tomorrow, does that sound okay to you?" Curtis asked.

"That would be great." Cathy nodded.

"About eight." He agreed. "The water should be warm enough by then."

"Thanks. It's not too last minute?" Cathy asked.

"Not at all. My schedule is pretty clear tomorrow."

"Okay, wonderful. We'll be there." Cathy nudged her brother with her elbow. "If he's brave enough that is."

"Oh, I'll be there all right." Ben shot a glare in her direction. "We'll see who goes in first."

"All right, it's not a competition." Curtis grinned. "It is best to have a healthy sense of caution. Diving can be dangerous. Am I right, Jim?" He nodded his head at his friend.

"Yes, that's for sure." Jim frowned. "Remember Bermuda?"

"That's just what I was thinking of, actually."

"What happened in Bermuda?" Suzie leaned closer. "I love a good story."

"I don't know if you could say that it was good. It was dangerous, and we were young, and stupid," Curtis said.

"Well, I was young, you were just stupid." Jim grinned.

"We both went down there, didn't we?"

"Yes, we did." Jim glanced around the table as everyone stared at him. "We were after treasure, how could we resist?"

"Treasure? Real treasure?" Ben's eyes widened.

"Sure. Left behind in a Spanish shipwreck. The dive was so dangerous that we had to go in secret, otherwise the authorities would have arrested us for trying. But we did it anyway." Curtis shook his head. "We came this close to running out of oxygen before we hit the surface." He held his fingers an inch apart. "A few minutes longer, and we would have both been dead."

"I haven't forgotten, Curtis, you were the one that pulled me up. Once I spotted the shipwreck, I wasn't going to turn back. I'm grateful to you every day for that, brother, you saved my life."

"The important thing is that we both made it out of there, which I can't say for other people that tried."

"Wow. But you actually found the shipwreck?" Ben scooted his chair forward. "Did you see the treasure?"

"No." Jim shrugged. "We didn't get close enough. The shipwreck was just too deep. It's impossible to get down there."

"So, the treasure could still be there? Wow!"

"I think the moral of the story, Ben, is that these two almost lost their lives chasing after that treasure. It wasn't worth it, was it guys?" Mary looked between Curtis and Jim.

"No, it wasn't." Jim frowned. "Was it Curtis?" He locked eyes with him.

"As tempting as it is to think of riches and wealth, the greatest treasure is having your life."

"Curtis is absolutely right." Mary smiled. "Which is why I trust him to teach you how to dive tomorrow. But you will be extra careful, right?"

"Absolutely." Ben smiled and took another bite of his food.

As the discussion continued Suzie thought about Hal and Trish. She hoped they'd had a good dinner and that the issues between them and Curtis didn't escalate. Luckily Hal and Trish would be leaving in a few days. At least that would prevent any drama from growing. After dinner Mary started clearing the dishes.

"No ma'am, that's my job." Suzie plucked the plates right out of her hands.

"Suzie! You have to let me help a little bit."

"I do not. You know telling me what to do never does any good."

"That's a good point, but you must be exhausted from everything today."

"I'm not really, I'm fine." She paused. "I am concerned about Hal and Trish though."

"Why is that?"

"There seems to be an issue between them and Curtis."

"Oh." Mary placed a hand over her lips and nodded.

"What is it?"

"Nothing." Mary picked up another plate.

Suzie took it from her hand and raised an eyebrow. "Oh no you're not getting away with that this time. You know something, so spill."

"Fine, I will, if you spill what Ben told you."

"He didn't mention anything?"

"No, he didn't. I want to know what's going on with him."

"Mary, you know I can't break his confidence. I wouldn't feel right about it, and if you're honest with yourself, you wouldn't feel right about it either."

"Yes, you're right I wouldn't. It's just driving me crazy not to know."

"He'll tell you when he's ready. If I thought he was in any danger I would tell you right away, you know that."

"I know." She sighed. "I'm glad he talked to you."

"So, are you going to spill?"

"It's just that I saw something the other night."

"Saw what?" Suzie gave up on trying to prevent Mary from clearing the table, and allowed her to carry a few glasses to the sink as they talked.

"I don't like to spread gossip, you know that, and I believe in people's privacy, but since this issue seems to be growing, I guess I should tell you."

"Yes, you should." Suzie raised an eyebrow. "What is it?"

"I saw Trish on the beach, and I was going to say hello to her, but she walked right up to Curtis. He was fishing, and didn't notice her at first I guess. She stood there behind him for a moment, then stepped up beside him. She tapped him on the shoulder, and when he turned, she kissed him."

"What? She didn't say anything to him?"

"Not that I saw."

"So she just walked up to him and kissed him?"

"That's what it looked like to me, but I was far away. Maybe I missed something."

"What did he do?"

"I don't know. When I saw that I ducked back into the house. I didn't want them to know that I saw. I thought that would be awkward."

"Very." Suzie sighed. "This could prove more troublesome than I thought. Maybe I will talk to Curtis about it."

"What are you going to do, say 'oh by the way please refrain from kissing our married guests'?"

"I don't know." Suzie shrugged. "We don't want guests that are causing problems, especially long term guests."

"Maybe it's Trish that caused the problem." Mary pursed her lips. "She's the one who walked up to him."

"That may be true, but Curtis should know better."

"Not everyone has the same set of morals though, that's something that I'm having to learn to accept." Mary frowned.

41

"Good point. I'll see if I can bring it up in a less intrusive way."

"Or maybe just let it rest for a day or two. They are leaving soon."

"Okay, I'll think about it. Now off with you, you're not washing a single dish."

"But I could dry..."

"No! Go be with your kids." She picked up a towel and snapped it in Mary's direction. "Now, I say!"

"Sorry, you're still not scary." Mary laughed as she walked out of the kitchen.

"Poor Hal," Suzie muttered to herself as she began to wash the dishes. She really had no idea how to approach Curtis about the issue. Was it even her place to? She could let it go as Mary suggested, but what if things grew more tense and a fight broke out? Without Jason around to help them out, they would have to turn to Kirk Rondella, Jason's partner on the police force, who wasn't nearly as flexible. He used to be in the army and was quite new to Garber. Suzie decided that she would leave it for the moment, but if it caused any problems she would speak to Curtis.

After Suzie went to bed that night she could hear Jim moving around in the room above hers. Something scraped across the floor. She wondered what it was, and did her best to ignore it. When the room became stuffy she opened her window halfway and heard Mary's voice drift up towards her. One glance down at the wraparound porch revealed that she was outside with Ben. She sighed with relief as she tucked herself back into bed. Maybe Ben would come clean.

**

Mary reached out and patted her son's knee. "You know there's nothing that you can't tell me, right?"

"I know, Ma."

"Do you?" She looked into his eyes. "Life is hard, Ben. I get that. Being an adult, well it's not

43

the greatest thing in the world, is it?"

"No." He sat back in the wooden deck chair. "It's not."

"So tell me, maybe I can help."

"Suzie talked to you, huh?"

"She only said that you needed to talk to me. She didn't tell me anything about why."

"All right, I guess it's better to get it out now. You're going to find out eventually."

"What is it?"

"I'm failing in school. I wasn't making ends meet, so I took on an extra job, I didn't think it would be a big deal, but I ended up being exhausted. I fell asleep in class a couple of times, the teacher got upset. So I ditched the extra job, but the bills keep coming in and…"

"But I send you money every month, it isn't enough?"

"I screwed up. I owe some people some money."

"What do you mean?" She studied him. "Tell me the details."

"I wanted to get a new computer, and some other things. I needed some extra cash. What you send me is a lot, but I just got caught up in this lifestyle. Most of my friends there are pretty well off, and they could always just get whatever they wanted. One of them suggested I go to his friend for a loan, just so I could get a few things, and then I could pay him off when your check came. But that's not what happened. I went to this guy for a loan, and he seemed nice enough, but it turned out he wasn't just friendly, he was doing this as a business. After he gave me the money he started hitting me up for interest, I had to give him my whole check from you. That's when I picked up the second job. But then the guy wanted more money, he said it wasn't enough. I was going to go to the police, but this guy is a real sketchy person. I'm just not sure what to do. He just keeps asking me for more. I've already paid him double what I borrowed."

"Ben. You should have told me about all of this from the beginning."

"I know." He sighed and ran his hands through his hair. "I know. I thought I could handle it. Every time I thought I had it handled, something would change. I know I should have just talked to you or Dad, but I wanted to see if I could fix it myself. I think the only way to fix it is to leave college."

"The only way you can fix this is if you bring up your grades. You're not leaving college."

"Mom."

"Ben, I mean it."

"I thought you said I could tell you about anything?"

"Yes, you can, but this is non-negotiable. You have to finish your education."

"The thing is, he knows where I live, in the dorms. Even if I pay him, he'll always be able to find me. I thought maybe dropping out would be the best idea. He'll forget all about me, and I can go back to school in a couple of years."

"That's not right. We're going to get the police involved in this."

"Mom, you can't. I have no idea what he'll do."

"Let me think about it. I'll figure something out. In the meantime, don't ever let yourself go without and land up in trouble. You could have asked me for extra money."

"I didn't want to have to tell you what I did, how stupid I was. I just wanted to be an adult and handle things."

"Sweetheart, being an adult doesn't always make you able to handle things. Trust me, I've been an adult for a long time, and I've faced a lot of bad situations. I don't always make the right decision, no one does. But you have someone to turn to when that happens, never forget that."

"I just don't want to put any extra pressure on you."

"You're not. I want to help you. We'll figure this out, together." She patted his knee again. "But not tonight. Let me sleep on it."

"Okay." He stood up, and turned back to offer her a hand.

"It's okay, I'm okay." As Mary pushed herself to her feet she did her best to hide the pain that washed through her knees. Lately it seemed to be getting worse. While Suzie was spry and always up to any physical challenge, Mary often felt that she'd aged beyond her years.

"Have you been to the doctor?"

"Yes honey, it's okay, it's just a bit of arthritis."

"It seems like more than that."

"It's not. Sometimes it's just been a long day, and I'm ready to rest."

"All right." He kissed her cheek and walked her to her room. As she closed the door to her bedroom, she leaned on it for support. It wasn't her knees that threatened to make her collapse, it was the thought of her son caught up in such a dangerous situation. How hadn't she known? Why did he think he needed to prove something to her by handling the situation all on his own? None of it made sense. She'd always tried to make herself completely available to her children. Maybe Dune House had distracted her, and she just didn't notice the change in him? She fell asleep, still troubled by what Ben revealed.

Chapter Four

Just as the sun peeked past the horizon, Suzie made her way into the kitchen. She expected to start the coffee, but heard the machine lid snap shut. There in the shadows, Mary turned the switch on the coffee pot and it began to brew.

"Morning Suzie."

"Morning. I guess we're both early risers today."

"Yes." Mary leaned back against the counter and frowned. "I had some trouble sleeping."

"Uh oh. Did Ben talk to you?"

"Yes, and I have no idea what to do."

"What's going on? He didn't tell me any details."

"He's gotten himself into trouble with some kind of loan shark. I'm not sure what to think at this point. He wants to drop out to get away from this guy who just keeps coming after him for more money."

"Why don't we have Jason look into it when he gets back?"

"Ben doesn't want me to, but I think I will. I'm not sure what Jason can do since it's out of his jurisdiction."

"That's true but maybe he can give us some advice about how to legally get Ben out of the situation."

"That's a good idea." Mary shook her head. "I think the thing that I'm upset about the most, is that he didn't come to me right away when he needed money instead of going to someone else. He says it was because he was trying to handle things as an adult. But I think it's because he worries about me."

"It's probably a little of both. He's a good young man, Mary. He'll get all of this straightened out, and everything will be fine."

"I sure hope so."

"What are your plans today?"

"Well, the kids have their lesson with Curtis, then afterwards I'm going to take them shopping. What about you?"

"It's supposed to be a nice morning. I'm going to work on decorating the front porch. I want to add a few splashes of color and stain some of the chairs that we have out there."

"Okay, do you want any help with it?" Mary asked.

"No thanks, I can handle it. Did the kids already go down to the beach to meet Curtis?"

"Not yet. I don't think they're up yet. But Curtis must already be down there. I didn't even see him leave this morning, but there is a light on in the shack."

"I'm going to have my coffee on the porch. Do you want to join me?"

"Yes, in a bit. I'll just wait for Cathy and Ben so they can have a coffee and bagel before they go diving. I doubt they'll want a big breakfast."

"Okay, I'll make breakfast for the others when they are up then I'll make a start on these projects. Oh, and if we don't hear from that locksmith today, then we need to call someone else. If Jason was here he'd fix it right up for us."

"So would Wes. Maybe we should ask Kirk?" Mary raised an eyebrow. "He might be willing to help."

"I don't know. I don't know Kirk that well, and though he seems like a good guy, I'm not so sure Jason would like us asking his partner for favors."

"All right, then let's just hope that the locksmith comes through today."

"If he doesn't, we can ask Paul when he docks. It is a bit of an inconvenience with the door being jammed."

Suzie headed out onto the back porch. A few minutes later Cathy made her way down the stairs.

"Morning Mom."

"Morning sweetie. Do you want some coffee and a bagel before you head out?"

"Sure." Cathy grabbed a mug from the cabinet. "You're up early."

"Oh, I'm usually up this early. I like to have a little time before the guests get up to tidy up, get some coffee brewing and enjoy the view."

"I can see why. This is a very beautiful place, Mom. Every time I visit it seems to get more beautiful."

"Yes, I honestly love it here."

"I'm glad. I was worried about you after the divorce."

"No need to worry, I'm okay now." Mary smiled. "Remember, it's my job to worry about you, not the other way around."

"I can worry a little, too."

"Just a little though." Mary filled Cathy's mug with coffee and handed her a buttered bagel.

"What about Rick? Is he just a boyfriend, or do you think he might be something more?"

"I'm in love with him, if that's what you mean. I'm just not so sure how he feels about me. It all happened so fast."

"Fast?"

"Yes, we met in class, and then we started spending every day together. When I decided to come here for a visit, he asked to come along so that he could meet you. That surprised me. Most young men want to avoid that kind of commitment so soon, right? But he was eager to meet you. I guess that's a good sign."

"It depends on the man." Mary smiled. "Maybe Rick is smart enough to see what an amazing woman he's with, and he doesn't want to take the chance of losing you. He's impressed me so far. But make sure you're taking the time to really get to know him. He certainly seems to be very fond of you."

"Maybe." She blushed as she glanced away. "I

can see a life with him. But it's a bit earlier than I expected. I thought I'd finish school before I even thought about marriage."

"You still can." Mary looked into her eyes. "A relationship is not about giving up your freedom or your choices, Cathy. If he loves you, he will wait until you're ready for more. Finish school, find your passion, and if the relationship is still going strong, then you will know it's worth considering marriage."

"Thanks Mom." She hugged her. "I'll keep that in mind."

"Cathy, are you ready to go?" Ben bounded into the kitchen. Mary smiled as his mannerisms still reminded her of the little boy that would run from room to room. He broke her rule about no running in the house because he simply could not walk. He ran everywhere, and she decided that it was not a battle that she needed to win.

"Yes, just grabbed a cup of coffee," Cathy said.

"Ben?" Mary held up the pot.

"No way, that stuff is toxic." He grabbed a small can out of the refrigerator.

"Sure, and that energy drink is full of all kinds of healthy things," Cathy said.

"At least it isn't ruining the environment," Ben said.

"You two don't start squabbling this early. Here's a bagel, Ben," Mary said as she handed it to him.

"Thanks, Mom."

"Go and have fun. Here, Cathy, take Curtis a bagel and a cup of coffee, too." She poured some coffee into a travel mug and handed it and a bagel over to Cathy. "Please be careful. I trust Curtis, but still, be careful."

"We will, Mom, don't worry." Ben kissed her cheek. Mary walked out with them through the front door. Then she made her way around to the side porch to watch as they raced each other down the beach. She was surprised at just how early

Curtis got up. He was always up early. She liked that about him. Most young people she knew wasted the morning. It could be such a peaceful and reflective time.

"Can I join you?" She paused beside the table where Suzie was seated.

"Of course you can, I've been waiting for you. I see that Cathy and Ben are up."

"Yes, they're already squabbling, too. I really thought that was something they would grow out of, I can't believe they're still at each other's throats."

"Just be glad that they're not coming to blows." Suzie laughed. "That would be a problem."

"That's for sure. I got more than one bruise pulling those two apart as kids. I guess since they're so close in age they fight about everything."

"That or they're two strong-willed, intelligent

people that are just as stubborn as their mother."

"Ouch." Mary laughed.

"Oh, you can play that sweet and docile role all you want, I remember the days when you would have knocked out anyone that challenged you."

"Knocked out is a bit strong." Mary grinned. "True, but strong."

"Oops, I'd better watch myself." Suzie laughed and looked out over the water. "I know we've both been through some hard times, but I'm so glad that we ended up here, like this. I never imagined it, but now I can't imagine living any other way."

"Me neither." Mary bit into her bottom lip. "Does that mean you're not going to marry Paul and move out?"

"What?" Suzie almost choked on her coffee. "Why would you have that idea?"

"I don't know, you two have gotten so close and he's always away..."

"And I like it that way. You know I don't want to get married," Suzie said. "I enjoy Paul, I would even go so far as to say that I'm fond of him, but our relationship works because we have space. I miss him when he's gone, I like missing him. It's better than being irritated that he's constantly underfoot."

"I see your point." Mary sipped her coffee. "But I imagine in another ten years or so he'll retire."

"He may." Suzie shrugged as she tucked her brassy blond hair behind her ear. "But a lot can happen in that time."

"That's true."

"I'm going to get breakfast ready, I'll make you something delicious, too."

"Oh good, I'm starving. With all the excitement my appetite is crazy."

"That's a good thing."

"If you say so." Mary patted her rounded

belly.

"I do." Suzie winked at her, then walked back around the house to the front door. She reached the kitchen in time to see Trish reach the bottom of the stairs.

"Good morning, Trish, there's some coffee if you'd like some."

"Yes, that would be great." Trish sighed and followed her into the kitchen. Suzie poured her a mug, then turned to hand it to her. When she saw Trish's face she was startled by how swollen and red her eyes were.

"Trish, are you all right?"

"Yes, I guess." She frowned. "I'm sorry, I know I'm a mess. Hal and I had a fight."

"He seems to have a bit of a temper."

"He really doesn't. But ever since we've been here, he hasn't been himself."

"Why do you think that is? Isn't he comfortable here with us?"

"Oh no, it's not you, not at all. Honestly, it's Curtis. Hal has a jealous streak. I tried to tell him that there was nothing to worry about, but he got so mad, and took off this morning. I have no idea where he went."

"It might be good for him to go somewhere and cool off. I'm so sorry that this is weighing on your time here."

"It's my fault really. I probably took things a little too far with Curtis. I'm getting older, and it's nice when a young man pays attention to me."

"It sounds like it's all a misunderstanding. Maybe if Hal and Curtis just talked about it…"

"No, I don't think that's a good idea. Hal already has it in his head that somehow I'm plotting against him. I think once we go home, everything will smooth out. We might end up leaving tomorrow instead of the next day, just so that we can get all of this straightened out."

"Well, that's a shame, but I understand. If there's anything I can do to help just let me know."

"Thanks Suzie. You really have done a great job of making us feel welcome. Hal is just out of sorts."

"If he does anything to hurt you..."

"He would never do anything like that. He has a loud bark, but zero bite."

"Sometimes people surprise you."

"That's true, but not Hal. He's just wound up because he's protective of me, and has always had this strange fear of losing me. I've tried to reassure him over the years, but it's never changed. Thanks for the coffee."

"I'm making breakfast."

"I'm not hungry, I'm sorry. I have no idea when Hal will be back either."

"Okay. There is plenty of food in the refrigerator if you get hungry later."

"Thanks Suzie."

As Trish walked away, Suzie wondered about what Mary saw on the beach. Was it possible that Trish was trying to make Hal jealous? The smell of smoke distracted her from her thoughts as the oil began to burn in the frying pan. She began to pour pancake batter into the frying pan. A few minutes later Mary stepped inside.

"Oh, that smells delicious."

"Well, I hope your appetite is still good because it's just going to be us, Jim and Rick."

"Speaking of." Rick grinned as he walked into the kitchen. "Good morning, ladies."

"Morning." Mary smiled at him. "Cathy's already gone down for her lesson."

"I know, I'm going to head down soon to see if I can observe."

"Please eat a pancake first, no one else wanted breakfast." Suzie grinned as she flipped a pancake.

"I wouldn't miss it for anything." He laughed.

Jim came down the stairs next. His hair was ruffled as if he'd just woken up.

"Morning Jim. Are you hungry?" Suzie began to slide pancakes onto a plate.

"Sure. Thanks." He sat down beside Rick. "So you didn't join in on the lesson?"

"No, as I said yesterday I'm already a trained diver."

"What do you do?"

"I'm in college at the moment." He smiled. "And you?"

"I guess you could say I'm a traveler." Jim laughed. "I travel all over the world to abseil, dive, and take on jobs in-between."

"That sounds like a very interesting life." Suzie sat down at the table with a plate of pancakes for everyone to choose from.

"It is. It's adventurous, that's for sure."

"Rick, how did you become a qualified diver?" Mary looked across the table at him.

"I was in the navy for a short time." He picked up his water and took a long swallow.

"Why so short?" Jim stabbed his pancakes with his fork.

"Uh, it was complicated. Let's just say, I didn't meet their needs. But I did learn how to dive." He smiled and shrugged. Mary narrowed her eyes. She couldn't help but wonder why her daughter's boyfriend would be kicked out of the navy. Was that even possible?

"Well, I'm sure Cathy and Ben are having a great time." Suzie smiled as she steered the conversation in a new direction.

"Yes, I'm going to go check on them then maybe head into town for a bit. Thanks for breakfast." Rick left the table.

"Oh Jim, I need to get your information for the room registration. I know that Curtis is covering the bill, but I still need to have your information in the system."

"Oh sure. I'll bring my wallet down in a little while. I've got some research to do, so I'm going to do it on my phone in my room."

"There's a local library that's great for that if you're interested. Curtis goes there a lot. The librarian, Louis is a research guru."

"Interesting. I'll keep that in mind. Thanks." Jim headed back upstairs.

"Okay, now I am cleaning this up and I won't hear a single argument from you." Mary pointed a finger at Suzie. "The kids won't be done with their lesson for a while, and I need something to keep my mind busy."

"All right, fine. But just this once." Suzie grinned as she stepped out through the back door. She went to the shed to get the supplies she needed. Then she set up shop on the front porch. As she began to select which furniture she wanted to stain, she immersed herself in the work.

Chapter Five

Mary finished the breakfast dishes, then began to cut some vegetables for lunch. She hummed under her breath as she worked.

"Cathy does that, too."

She jumped at the sound of Rick's voice and turned to look at him. "Oh, I didn't know you were there."

"I'm sorry, I didn't mean to startle you. It's just, now I see where she gets it from. Whenever she's working on something, she hums."

"Oops, I guess I gave her my bad habit." Mary laughed.

"I don't think it's bad at all." He plucked a slice of pepper off the cutting board. "Do you mind?"

"No, go ahead."

"I'm just heading out. I'm going to explore the area a little."

"When the kids get back, and after they've rested if they want to, I'm going to take everyone down to the local shops. There are very nice places to browse."

"Oh great, I'm looking forward to that. I'll make sure I stay close by."

"If you need anything just give me a call."

"Thanks." Rick hesitated. "I'm sorry, I'm not sure what I should call you."

"Mary is fine." She offered him a warm smile.

"Thanks Mary."

After he left she returned to chopping the vegetables. She did like how polite he was. She could only hope that charm was genuine.

Just before lunch the door swung open and Cathy stepped inside.

"Cathy!" Mary smiled at her. "How did it go?"

"It was great. I learned so much. I can't wait to go diving with Rick. It'll be fun."

"Do you feel like you are ready to go out on your own?"

"No, not on my own, but with Rick there I'll be just fine. I think the hardest part is trying to figure out the equipment. Curtis made it seem so simple, but I don't know if I'd trust that I got it just right."

"I can understand that fear. I think you're brave enough just for going down there. Did you see anything amazing?"

"I saw things I never could have imagined and if you told me they were real, I would have argued the point. I had no idea what was swimming in the water before. I know that you're not interested in doing it, but if you ever wanted to, it would be worth it just to see the magnificent creatures."

"I think I'll stick to pictures, and the descriptions you give."

"I don't blame you." Cathy grinned. "When we turned around to surface and I realized how deep we were I almost panicked. Luckily Curtis was there to guide me."

"What about Ben? How did he handle it? Where is he anyway?"

"He liked it, too. I think he chased after some girls on the beach. He's gotten to be a bit of a flirt."

"Ugh, I don't think I want to know that."

"Don't worry, Mom, he's a good guy. He's just excited to have a girlfriend."

"Girlfriends, boyfriends." Mary shook her head. "I remember when you both were in diapers."

"Mom!"

"All right, I'm sorry." Mary laughed. "I know that you're both grown up, and I'm happy that you can be with people that make you happy."

"Speaking of that, have you seen Rick?"

"He went out about a half hour ago. He said he wouldn't be far. I told him I wanted to go shopping this afternoon. After lunch."

"Hmm, maybe he texted me." She rummaged in her purse for her phone. After she checked it she shook her head. "No texts."

"Maybe he just ran to the store for something. He said he wanted to explore."

"It's odd for him to go without me."

"It seems your brother is occupied, so I guess he's not going to want to go out. What about you?"

"I don't know, Mom. I think I'd rather just lay down for a little while. That adventure wore me out. Plus, I want to wait for Rick to get back. Then we could all go out together."

"Okay. Are you ready for some lunch?"

"I could eat." She grinned.

"Okay, go rest for about fifteen minutes, then everything should be ready."

"Thanks, Mom."

As Mary began to set out plates for all of the guests, she smiled at the thought of what came next for her family. Would there be weddings?

Grandchildren? Sure, she wouldn't want either of her children to rush into things. Those events were still years down the line, but she took pleasure in the thought of them. Once lunch was ready she rang the bell to announce it. Trish and Jim came downstairs, and a few minutes later Cathy followed. Mary stuck her head out on to the front porch and smiled at Suzie.

"Time to take a break and have some lunch."

"What do you think?" Suzie stepped aside from one of the rocking chairs she'd stained.

"Wow, that's beautiful. It's the perfect color. I love light blue."

"Thanks." Suzie sighed and wiped her hand across her forehead. "It was a bit more of a project than I expected. I'll go wash up."

"Come eat." She opened the door for Suzie and started to follow her, but froze when she saw Ben run up the porch steps towards her. His expression caused her heart to drop. Something terrible had happened.

"Mom! Mom!" Ben ran up to her, covered in sand, his cheeks red from exertion.

"Ben, what is it? What's wrong?"

"It's Curtis! He just washed up on the beach!"

"What?" Mary's chest heaved as she tried to make sense of what her son said. "What are you talking about?"

"I was walking down the beach and I saw all kinds of flashing lights. When I got close enough, I saw him on the beach. It's Curtis, and he's dead, Mom. He's dead!"

"Oh Ben!" She wrapped her arms around him and pulled him close. As strong as he was, she could feel him quake in her grasp.

"I just saw him this morning, Mom. How could he be dead?"

"Maybe there's some mistake."

"No, there's no mistake, I saw him myself. He still had his diving equipment on."

"Oh, how horrible." Mary fought back tears as

74

she hugged her son again. "I'm so sorry that you saw that."

"Let's just go inside, Mom, I don't want to think about it anymore."

"All right, come on in." She stared down the beach in the direction her son ran from. In the distance she could see the glimmer of flashing lights. When she opened the door to Dune House she found Rick and Cathy snuggled together on the couch. He must have returned at some point, and she didn't notice. "Suzie! Suzie?"

"She just went out through the back. I think she was going to lock up the shed. Ben, what's wrong? Mom? You're white as a sheet!"

"It's Curtis!" Ben blurted out the words as he stumbled further into the room. "They just found him on the beach. Dead."

"Dead?" Cathy jumped up from the couch. "Are you sure?"

"Yes, I saw him." Ben wiped at his eyes.

"How could this happen?" Cathy shuddered. Rick stood up and wrapped an arm around her shoulders.

"Accidents do happen, Cathy. Diving can be dangerous," Rick said.

"But Curtis was an expert. How could something like this happen to him?" Cathy shook her head.

Mary walked through the kitchen to the back door. She spotted Suzie fighting with the lock on the shed. "Suzie! Come in, I need to tell you something."

"Just a second, this lock is stuck."

"Suzie, please, you have to come inside now!"

Suzie let go of the lock and turned to look at her. "What is it, Mary?" She jogged up to the back door and Mary led her into the house.

"Curtis is dead. They found him on the beach. I'm not sure what's happened yet, but I know that he is dead."

"Oh, that's terrible! I can't believe it's true." Suzie's eyes filled with tears. "He was so young, and such a nice person! How could this happen?"

"The police are down there now, trying to figure that out." Mary frowned. "I wish Jason was here to handle this. I like Kirk, but I trust Jason."

"I agree. But Kirk is the one that is here, so we'll just have to see how he handles it. I'm sure he'll do a good job." Suzie crossed her arms as she stared off into space for a moment. "Do you think it was an accident?"

"I would assume it could only be. Maybe he dove too long, or maybe he had some kind of medical problem under the water."

"But he was so young and healthy. I doubt he could have had any medical problems."

"Maybe not but it's possible. Maybe drugs?" Mary frowned. "I hate to think he might have been using them, but maybe?"

"Maybe." Suzie sighed. "There's no point in

guessing. I'm sure the police will be along to collect his things from his room. What a terrible, terrible, thing." Suzie clutched the slope of her neck. "Have you told the kids yet?"

"Yes, they already know. Ben saw him."

"Poor thing. I'm sorry this happened, Mary. I know you were looking forward to having a great time with the kids, and now it seems that might not happen."

"I just can't believe that Curtis is gone."

"Neither can I." Suzie blinked and shook her head. "It seems impossible. I'm going to walk down there and find out what's happening."

"All right, maybe that's a good idea." Mary wrung her hands. "I have no idea what to do."

"Just stay with the kids. They need you right now."

Chapter Six

Suzie stepped out onto the front porch. When she saw the patrol car pull up in front of Dune House, she wasn't surprised. She was certain that Kirk would have some questions and want to take a look at Curtis' things, perhaps to contact next of kin.

When Kirk stepped out of the car his expression was grave. She studied him as he walked up the steps and onto the porch. There was something about his expression that made her uneasy. It was more than sorrow. Was it suspicion?

"Hi Suzie." He leaned against the railing and rested one hand on his hip. "I guess you've heard?"

"Yes, I have, what a tragedy." She shook her head. The screen door squeaked as Mary pushed it open and stepped out onto the porch as well.

"Kirk, how are you holding up?"

"I'm fine." He reached up and pulled off his hat to reveal his shaved head. He toyed with the brim as he looked at the two women. "I'm just trying to gather some information."

"What kind of information?" Suzie raised an eyebrow. "Do you want his things from his room?"

"No, actually I'd prefer it if everyone stays out of his room. The crime scene investigation team will be here in a little while. They're still at the beach so it will take them some time to get out here."

"Crime scene investigation team?" Mary's eyes widened. "Is that really necessary?"

"Yes, I think it is." He looked between them nervously.

"Kirk, what is it? Just come out with it already. I can tell you have something to say." Suzie crossed her arms and locked her eyes to his.

"All right then. I don't think this was an

accident. I think it was a murder."

"But wasn't he diving alone?"

"Honestly, I'm not sure. We are waiting for the tests to confirm our suspicions, but from our initial investigations we believe that one of the cylinders that he had on was filled with something other than the oxygen mix used in diving tanks. He had two on. The first one was empty, I'm guessing, he did a long dive, then when the second one kicked in, whatever was inside killed him. They were new tanks. I contacted the company and they were delivered this morning. They were empty so he must have filled them this morning. I am certain an experienced diver would have checked his tanks to be sure they were filled properly. If he'd been close enough to the surface when he realized the problem, he would have been able to come up for air. It seems to me that someone wanted to make sure that he was deep enough that he had no chance. The tainted cylinder is almost completely empty." He narrowed his eyes. "There was no way he could have survived."

"There's no way Curtis would make a mistake like that." Suzie frowned. "He was impeccable with his equipment."

"So I've been told by a few of his students. Which is why I've come to the conclusion that there might be something far more sinister at play here. I will need to talk to both of you, as well as anyone else who is staying here."

"Of course. There's Trish and Hal, and Curtis' friend, Jim."

"And?" He looked over at Mary. "I was told that Curtis had some students this morning. Your son and daughter?"

"Well yes, but they're just here for a visit."

"If they had contact with the victim then I will need to talk with them." He set his jaw and held her gaze.

"Talk with them about what exactly?" Mary's

voice grew tense.

"I want to get everyone's whereabouts to see who has an alibi and who doesn't first of all, and secondly I want to know if anyone noticed anything strange about Curtis this morning."

"Alibis?" Suzie narrowed her eyes. "Now that's a stretch. None of us would have anything to do with Curtis' death."

"I'm sure that you know it's just routine. Everyone who has had contact with the victim needs to be questioned. I know this is going to be uncomfortable, and you're used to Jason being more flexible..."

"Now, wait a minute, Jason always does his job." Suzie frowned.

"He just knows better than to waste his time accusing people who had nothing to do with a murder." Mary shook her head. "My kids had nothing to do with any of this. They're already shaken up."

"Hold on, that's not what I'm saying. I'm sorry they're upset, but they're part of this investigation. They may have been the last ones to see Curtis alive." He straightened up and looked from one woman to the other. "I will do my job, understand? I have no interest in stepping on anyone's toes. But if you're not going to be cooperative then we are going to have a problem."

"A problem?" Suzie clenched her teeth for a moment, then took a breath. "All right. Mary, he's right. He's just trying to do his job. It will be a few questions, and that will be that. Of course we want to help figure out what happened to Curtis. Have you been able to reach any family members?"

"I'm afraid not. From the background check I did on him, I haven't found any living relatives, so there may not be any to find. In which case, I'm really going to need to gather as much information from you and Mary as possible. I know you don't know me as well as Jason, but I can assure you that anything I investigate is going to be done by the book, and in the pursuit of justice."

"That's very reassuring, Kirk. I'm sure you'll do a great job. Just try to remember that this has been very difficult for us as well. Curtis has been here for quite some time, and my kids just had a class with him this morning. Ben even saw him on the beach when he was pulled out of the water." Mary winced and shook her head. "I'm sorry if I overreacted, this is emotional for me, too. We both really enjoyed having Curtis here."

"Of course." Kirk put his hand on her shoulder. "I'm not here to cause more distress. I want this solved, just like you do."

"Just like we all do." Suzie nodded.

"I'll need to interview both of you as well." Kirk looked from Mary to Suzie.

"Of course, come inside." As Suzie stepped through the door with Mary right behind her, she noticed Trish approach from the stairs.

"What's going on?" Trish looked at Suzie with wide eyes. "I saw the police car out front."

Kirk stepped in behind Mary and pulled the door closed. "Did you know Curtis Malcolm?"

Trish looked between Suzie and Mary. "What's happened?"

"Curtis is dead, Trish, they found him on the beach." Mary frowned. "Kirk is here to investigate."

"What? Curtis is dead?" Trish's hand flew to her mouth to cover a gasp. "How?"

"It looks as if it was a homicide. I would like to ask you a few questions please?" Kirk gestured to the small study off the living room.

"Yes, of course. But I should tell my husband." She began to type on her phone.

"Is he nearby?"

"I have no idea where he is. He took off this morning and..." Trish stopped mid-sentence. "I mean, I'm sure he just went to the store for something."

"All right, let's just get started. I'll want to speak with him as well, when he's available." Kirk led her into the study and closed the door behind him.

"This is awful." Mary peeked into the living room where Rick, Cathy, and Ben were gathered.

"I wonder if she'll tell him?" Suzie crossed her arms. "About the kiss."

"I didn't even think about that. Hal was so angry with them both. What if he had something to do with this?"

"I don't want to jump to any conclusions. But it's possible. I doubt Trish is going to tell Kirk about any of it. We might have to be the ones to do it."

"I'd hate to cause a problem if Hal wasn't involved."

"I would, too, but this isn't about us, or Hal and Trish, it's about Curtis."

Mary nodded, then bit into her bottom lip.

"Someone has to tell Jim." Suzie stood close to Mary. "I don't think he should hear it from Kirk first. He may be a good police officer, but he's not very delicate."

"I haven't seen him since breakfast. He went back upstairs after breakfast and he hasn't come down since."

"Do you think he's okay?" Suzie asked.

"Well, he has to be up there, right? You haven't seen him since breakfast have you?"

"No and I've been on the front porch all morning. I'll go check on him." Suzie started up the stairs, but just as she set her foot on the bottom step she saw Jim at the top of the stairs. "Jim. You should come down here. Something terrible has happened."

"What is it?" He pounded down the rest of the stairs and paused at the bottom, just as Kirk stepped out of the study.

"Jim Smithsy?" Kirk locked eyes with the other man.

"Yes, I'm Jim. What is this about?" He frowned.

"I'm sorry to inform you of this. Your friend Curtis has passed away."

"What?" Jim grabbed the railing on the stairs and did his best to steady himself. Suzie grabbed his other arm to offer him some support.

"I'm so sorry, Jim."

"You two were friends for a long time?" Kirk studied him.

"Years." Jim straightened up and closed his eyes. "How did he die?"

"I believe he was murdered."

"You believe he was, or he was?" Jim stared at him.

"At this time there is evidence to support that there was foul play involved in his death. However, the investigation is ongoing."

"I don't understand. How can you not know if a person was murdered or not?"

"He died because of a problem with his equipment. Can you tell me where you were this morning between eight and twelve-thirty?"

"A problem with his equipment?" Jim shook his head. "I was here. I went back upstairs after breakfast, did some research and then I fell asleep. I just woke up a little while ago and heard the commotion."

"Suzie?" Kirk looked over at her. "Can you confirm that?"

"I was on the porch all morning, and Mary was in the kitchen. The lock on the side door is jammed so the door can't be opened. If Jim had left, I would have seen him go through the front, or Mary would have seen him go through the back."

"All right, thank you." He made a note, then looked back at Jim. "Do you mind if we talk for a few minutes? I'd like to know as much as I can about Curtis."

"Yes." Jim closed his eyes. "I'll tell you whatever I can. I can't believe he's dead. This is so surreal."

"I can assure you, Jim, I will do whatever has to be done to make sure that Curtis' killer is found. I'm very sorry for your loss." Kirk led Jim away from the staircase to the study. As he closed the door, Mary shivered.

"Poor man. He lost a good friend. I should check on the kids."

"Yes." Suzie nodded as Mary walked past her to the living room. She leaned against the wall and closed her eyes. Where was Hal? Had he tampered with Curtis' equipment and then taken off? It made her very uncomfortable to think that she might have allowed a killer to stay under their roof. Getting the guest's details didn't really give them much information about them. That thought reminded her that she had never registered Jim in the computer system. She dismissed it as unimportant now. She doubted he would be staying long.

Chapter Seven

Suzie couldn't stop thinking about Curtis. To distract herself she put a few things together in the kitchen and carried the tray out into the living room. Everyone stared at the crackers and cheese as if they might be foreign objects. Suzie set the tray down on the coffee table and sank down into a chair.

"I know this is going to be hard on all of you, but Kirk is going to want to speak to all of us. It's important that he has all of the information that we can give him, even if you don't think it's important," Mary said.

"Mom, I don't want to talk to a cop." Ben rubbed his hands along his knees and frowned.

"Ben, it's okay. We know Kirk, he's a good guy, and he'll treat everyone fairly."

"No." Ben looked into his mother's eyes. "What if I say something wrong?"

"It's not a test, Ben, you just tell the truth." Cathy rolled her eyes.

"Cathy, be nice. This is stressful for everyone," Mary said.

"It's okay, Ben," Cathy said. "There's nothing to worry about. It's not like you killed him."

"Of course I didn't." Ben scowled. "That doesn't mean I'm okay with being questioned by the police."

"Relax hon, I'll go in with you. With both of you." Mary looked at Cathy. "I think that would be best."

"Mom, it's not really necessary." Cathy sighed. "We're not little kids."

"I know that, but when it comes to something like this, it's just best to be cautious."

"Ben? Could I speak with you?" Kirk stood in the doorway of the living room.

"I'm going to join him." Mary stood up.

"That's fine." Kirk nodded. "Whatever makes

you comfortable."

Mary followed Ben into the study with Kirk and sat down beside him. She was relieved that Kirk hadn't fought her on it.

"I don't know what I can really tell you." Ben shrugged.

"Sometimes there are details that can be helpful to the case, that seem unimportant to you. So first, I'd like to know where you were between eight and twelve-thirty."

"From eight until a little after eleven we were with Curtis, taking his class."

"We?" Kirk glanced up from his notepad.

"Me, and my sister Cathy. Curtis was fine when we left him."

"What time do you think that was?"

"About eleven-fifteen, maybe? I wasn't really paying attention to the time."

"Okay, and where did you go after that?"

"I stayed out on the beach." He cleared his throat. "I saw some girls I wanted to try to talk to."

"And?"

"And what?"

"Did you talk to them?"

"What does that matter?" Ben frowned.

"If you spoke to them, then I can check with them to solidify your alibi."

"No, I didn't talk to them. I was too shy."

"Okay. What about anyone else? Did you speak to anyone who might be able to confirm your alibi?"

"I don't need an alibi. I didn't kill him."

"Ben, I'm not accusing you. It's just easier if I know where everyone was at what time. Just try to understand I'm here to help solve a crime not to cause problems."

"All right, I'm sorry. No, I didn't speak to anyone. I just walked around some. Then I got hungry and decided to come back here. As I was walking back, I saw Curtis being pulled out of the water." He winced.

"What about the time that you spent with Curtis? Do you remember anything strange about it?"

"Strange how?"

"Anything. Was he frustrated, did he mention any problems he was having, did anyone show up that wasn't supposed to be there?"

"No, I don't think so. I don't know." Ben frowned. "We were near the shore when some cylinders were dropped off and he just waved to the guy."

"If there's something you would like to tell me about Curtis, now is the time. I need as much information as I can get." Kirk leaned forward and tried to meet his eyes.

"It's okay, Ben, you can tell him the truth." Mary patted her son's hand.

"I don't know if it even matters. But during our lesson, before we got into the water, Curtis got a phone call. He seemed a little upset. He said that he was in the middle of a lesson and he didn't want to deal with whatever it was right then, and hung up the phone."

"Do you have any idea who he was talking to? A man, a woman? Did he say a name?"

"No. That's why I didn't know if I should mention it. He just went back to teaching us, but his demeanor changed. He wasn't laughing as much. I just figured someone got under his skin, but he tried to focus on the safety lesson he was giving us."

"It's good that you told me. I can check his phone records to see who called him." He made a note, then looked back at Ben. "I need you to be honest with me. Had you ever met Curtis before coming here to visit your mother?"

"No, I'd never met him before. He seemed like a nice guy though."

"During your lesson was there anything that came up between you and Curtis, or Curtis and your sister?"

"No, nothing at all. We had a good lesson. I enjoyed it, and so did Cathy."

"If you think of anything, anything at all, I want you to call me." He handed Ben a business card. "Even if it seems trivial, or unimportant, understand?"

"Yes." Ben nodded as he took the card and tucked it into his wallet. Kirk walked him to the door.

"Could you ask your sister to step in?"

"Sure, I will." He paused and looked at Mary. "Are you going to stay?"

"Yes." She met Kirk's eyes. "If you don't mind."

"Not at all." Kirk waited until Cathy stepped into the study. "Hi Catherine, I just want to ask you a few questions about your time with Curtis."

"But I barely knew him." She sat down next to Mary and took her mother's hand. "I don't know how I can help."

"You might be able to remember something that could help us with the case. Was there anyone else in the water with you?"

"No, there was no one else out there with us."

"What about on the beach? Did you see anyone walking? Any joggers? Anyone else?"

"Oh well, just Hal."

"Hal? Trish's husband?" Kirk made a note.

"Yes, when we were about to go into the water he walked past. Curtis was in the middle of giving us an instruction when Hal muttered something, he turned around to look at him."

"What did Hal say?"

"I didn't hear it. I was almost under the water, and Ben already was."

"What did Curtis do?"

"He didn't do anything. He just stared at him for a minute, then got back to the lesson."

"Do you think Hal's comment upset him?"

"Maybe surprised him?" Cathy frowned. "I don't know for sure. He didn't say anything about it."

"What about anything else? Did Curtis talk to you about anything personal?"

"Nothing that would matter." Cathy shrugged.

"Let me be the judge of that." He leaned forward and looked into her eyes. "What did you and Curtis talk about?"

"Not much." Cathy glanced over at her mother.

"It's okay, honey. Tell him whatever you talked about. It's important not to leave out a single detail."

"Well, like I said, it's not important. I'm a History major in college, and he asked me if I had any knowledge about artifacts, ancient culture, that kind of thing."

"And that didn't strike you as odd?"

"Not really. He'd mentioned that he was a bit of a treasure hunter, most deep sea divers are I guess. I figured he was interested in understanding how to tell the age of things so he could value them. I arranged to meet him at the library this evening to go over some websites that I thought might be helpful."

"What time were you supposed to meet?"

"Around seven." She took a deep breath. "I don't know how someone can just be gone like this. I'm sorry, I just can't believe it."

"It's difficult, I know." Kirk cleared his throat. "So did he mention what he wanted to value? Jewelry? Sculptures?"

"No, I asked him, but he said he didn't want to talk about it too much out in the open. I thought that was a little odd, but the lesson was over, and he hurried off."

"Did he say he had somewhere to be?"

"No, but he did look at his watch, and then he walked away fast, you know, like he was running late."

"Interesting. Thank you, Catherine, you've been very helpful. If you think of anything else that you think might have some bearing on the case, please contact me right away." He handed her a business card. "Anytime."

"Okay, I will." She frowned. "I hope you figure out who did this."

"Oh, I will." He stood up and straightened his shirt. As Cathy stepped out of the study, he turned back to Mary. "Where is Hal?"

"I have no idea. I'm sure Trish filled you in on their argument?"

"No, she didn't mention any argument." He narrowed his eyes.

"Oh."

"What about it, Mary?"

"Trish and Hal were having a bit of a spat."

"About what?"

"Curtis, I assume." Mary sighed. "Please understand, I'm sure Hal had nothing to do with Curtis' death."

"You can't be sure, can you? You barely know him."

"Maybe you're right. Hal was jealous over Curtis and Trish flirting. Curtis gave them lessons when he first arrived. He's friendly to all of his students. He was just a naturally friendly person. I think maybe Trish took it the wrong way. Or maybe Hal did. I don't really know. All I know is that they were arguing about it yesterday, and this morning he took off, and hasn't been back since."

"How far did things go between Curtis and Trish?"

"I'm not sure if Hal knows how far."

"But you do?" He rubbed a hand along his

cheek and took a breath. "I know, you don't want to get Trish into trouble. I'm not going to reveal more than I have to, but I need to know what was going on between Trish and Curtis."

"I think I saw her kiss him."

"You think you did?"

"It was at a distance, and I don't see very well far away. But it did look like she kissed him. She kind of, surprised him, from what I could tell."

"So he didn't initiate it?"

"Not from what I saw."

"After you saw this, did you see them together alone again?"

"No, I didn't."

"When she kissed him, did he talk to her for a while, or walk away?"

"I don't know, I went inside. I didn't want to be nosy."

"Okay." He made a note on his notepad. "I'm

sure you understand that it is important I get in touch with Hal. If he's done this, he could already be on the run. So if you hear anything about him, or see him, I need you to contact me right away. Can I trust you to do that?"

"Of course you can."

"Great. I'm going to need you to be on my side with this. As I see it right now, we have quite a few suspects to look at, and the only ones with an alibi are Jim and Trish."

"Are you saying you still consider my kids suspects?"

"I don't know what kind of motive they could have for killing Curtis, but yes technically they are still suspects because they have no alibi for the time-span that Curtis could have been killed in."

"But that time-span includes time when he was still alive."

"I'm aware. Because, at any point during that time someone could have tampered with his equipment. Without more information I have no idea when the killer accessed Curtis' tanks. It could have happened any time after they were dropped off and before he went diving, well for the final time."

"I can assure you my children had nothing to do with this."

"I believe you, Mary, I do. But I wouldn't be doing my job if I didn't investigate all avenues. I may know you, but I do not know your children. Until I am able to cross them off the list, I would appreciate it if they remained in this area."

"They're here to visit for a few days."

"Good. And, Hal and Trish?"

"They're supposed to leave first thing tomorrow."

"I'm going to have to prevent that. First, I need to track down Hal. Thanks for your time, Mary, I do appreciate you speaking with me."

"You're welcome, Kirk." She watched him

leave the study. Her legs weren't strong enough for her to stand up. Not because of pain, but because of Kirk's revelation that her children were murder suspects. How could she accept that? How could she explain that to them? Her stomach twisted with fear. What if Kirk got everything wrong? What if he found out about Ben's financial problems and somehow twisted that into a motive? Anxiety built within her the more she thought about the possibilities. As she stepped out of the study she saw Kirk head straight for Suzie.

"Can I speak to you for a minute?"

"Sure." Suzie stepped to the side with Kirk.

"I really need to find Hal, any idea where he is?"

"No, but I do have his license plate on file. Will that help?"

"Immensely."

"I'll get it for you."

"Could you run me a copy of Jim's

information as well?"

"I don't have it yet. He was supposed to give it to me today."

"All right, I'll get it from him. And Rick?" He glanced around. "Where is he?"

"He took Cathy out on the porch."

"I'm going to want to talk to him, too."

"I understand. I think they're on the side porch, if you want to head out there I'll bring you Hal's information."

"Okay great, thank you." Kirk stepped out through the door just as Hal was stepping in.

"May I ask your name, sir?"

"Hal Richson. Is there a problem, Officer?"

"I need to speak with you about a very important matter."

"What's happened? Is Trish okay? Trish?"

"I'm fine, Hal." She stepped out of the living room.

"I'll tell you everything you need to know. Just come with me please." Kirk led Hal into the study.

"I should go in there with him, shouldn't I?" Trish looked at Suzie.

"I think he'll be all right by himself. It's probably best if you let Kirk speak with him alone."

"Maybe." Trish frowned and lingered near the door to the study. Suzie finished printing off what information she had, then stepped outside to find Cathy and Rick. On her way out she overheard Mary and Ben as they spoke in the living room.

"Mom, I didn't have anything to do with it, you know that right?"

"Of course I do. There's nothing to worry about. I'm sure Kirk will get all of this figured out."

Chapter Eight

Suzie walked around to the side porch, and paused when she heard raised voices.

"I didn't come here to deal with the police. I don't handle that well, you know that. I think we should leave."

"I'm not going to leave my mom here to deal with all of this. There's nothing to worry about. Just tell him where you were, and everything will be fine."

"I shouldn't have to. I don't want to answer any questions. You can stay if you want to, I can understand that, but I'm leaving."

"If you do that you're going to make yourself look guilty."

"It won't matter if they can't catch me, will it?"

"Rick, this isn't like you. What's going on? You can talk to me."

"No, I can't. I have to get out of here. I'm

calling a cab." He pulled out his phone. Suzie ducked back around the corner and sent Kirk a text.

Rick is about to run. You need to get out here before he does.

Suzie felt a pang of guilt for putting Cathy's boyfriend in the crossfire, but with his behavior she had to wonder whether he might have something to hide.

"Rick please, just calm down. My mom knows the cops here, nothing bad is going to happen to you."

"You don't know that. Yes, I need a cab to Dune House right away." He turned away as he spoke on the phone. Suzie didn't even receive a text back, instead she heard the front door of Dune House swing open, and Kirk rounded the corner of the porch.

"Rick?" He paused in front of him. "Rick, we're going to need to talk."

"He doesn't know anything." Cathy stood up from her chair. "He had nothing to do with any of this."

"All I need is to clear my list of people that had contact with Curtis. That's it, Rick. Please, hang up the phone, I need to speak with you."

Rick shoved his phone into his pocket. He turned to look at Kirk with a scowl. "I don't have to speak to you. I know my rights."

"Okay Rick. Is there a reason you're feeling threatened? Have I done something to upset you?" Kirk asked.

Suzie stepped out to join them and placed a reassuring hand on Cathy's shoulder.

"I have a problem." Rick gritted his teeth. "I don't deal well with authority."

"Oh, I see." Kirk nodded. "Well relax. I'm not here to force you into anything. I'd just like to know if you thought Curtis was into anything he shouldn't have been? If you noticed anyone suspicious? Did you notice him arguing with anyone?"

"No, I barely spoke to him."

"Is that so? Because, I just had someone tell me that they saw you in a heated exchange with Curtis earlier today."

"What?" Cathy shook her head. "Rick didn't even speak to Curtis today. Right Rick?"

"Is that right, Rick?" Kirk's tone remained placid. "I just need all of the information I can get."

"Yes, I spoke to him."

"When?" Cathy stared at him.

"Cathy, let Kirk ask the questions." Suzie patted her shoulder.

"But I don't understand. You were still asleep when I left for the lesson with Curtis. When did you talk to him?" Cathy asked.

"Look, it isn't what you think. I went down there to check on things. I wanted to make sure that Curtis was taking care of Cathy and Ben. They were doing exercises under the water, when I saw Curtis come back up. He left the water to make a phone call! He left Cathy and Ben in the water by themselves, with equipment they weren't familiar with. I got upset, I told him that was against regulations and he needed to get back in the water. He argued with me, said he just needed to make a quick call, and they weren't that deep. But anything can happen in a second. I told him to get back in the water or I'd break his phone."

"So you threatened him?" Kirk narrowed his eyes.

"I was worried about Cathy and Ben."

"Did he listen to you?"

"Yes, he went back in the water, but I think he sent a text first."

"Do you remember that, Catherine? A time when Curtis left you alone in the water?" Kirk turned to look at her.

"Yes, I do. It was about fifteen minutes after we started out in the water. He motioned that he was going up, but Ben and I were fine and Curtis was back almost right away. Rick, why didn't you tell me about this?"

"I haven't had the chance."

"What did you do after you sent Curtis back into the water?"

"I left."

"So you were worried about Catherine's safety, but not enough to stick around?" Kirk asked.

"I didn't want her to know that I snapped at Curtis, all right? I was afraid she'd be upset with me."

"Rick, it's okay," Cathy said.

"Rick, you've helped me out a lot here. Can you tell me what you did after you left the beach?"

"I checked out the town. Walked around for a while."

"Did you meet anyone? Eat anywhere? Is there anyone who can verify where you were?"

"No, I was trying to blow off some steam, not make friends. I doubt anyone would remember seeing me, but maybe someone from one of the shops saw me from inside, I didn't go into any shops though."

"All right, listen. Stick around. Okay?" Kirk asked.

"Why? So you can arrest me? I know how these things work."

"Not like that they don't. I guarantee you I will only be putting handcuffs on the murderer. But if I need to be able to reach you to confirm something, or find out more information, and you're not here, that's going to cause me a lot of problems. Besides, this is supposed to be time with your girlfriend right? So why not stick around and keep her company."

"I think that would be best, Rick. Please?" Cathy met his eyes.

"All right, yes, I'll stay as long as we planned. But I can't promise anything beyond that."

"Great. Thanks Rick." Kirk offered his hand. "I appreciate it."

"Sure." Rick shook his hand.

"I'll cancel the taxi." Cathy smiled.

Suzie and Kirk walked back around to the front porch. The crime scene van drove into the parking lot as they paused by the front door.

"What about Hal, Kirk?"

"I've spoken with him. I've spoken with everyone here. Now, I'm going to let the crime scene team do their work."

"Okay." Suzie nodded.

"Please call me if you think of anything."

"Wait, Kirk."

"Yes?" He turned back to look at her.

"Do you think we're safe here?"

"Do you?" He stared back at her and squinted

through the sunlight. "Is there something you're not telling me, Suzie?"

"No, nothing."

"All right then. You should be just fine. But if anything worries you, call me right away."

"I will." She watched him return to the patrol car. A shudder ran down her spine. Was she going to be sharing a roof with a killer? Mary stepped outside and joined her on the porch.

"Is Kirk leaving?"

"Yes. He said to call him if we think of anything. The crime scene team is going to go through Curtis' room."

"What do you think, Suzie? Who do you think did this?"

"Honestly, it might not have even been anyone that we know. It could have been someone in town, or one of his other students."

"That's possible."

"I think it's more likely to be Hal though. I bet

119

he wanted to get revenge for the way that Curtis flirted with Trish." Suzie frowned.

"Or it could have been Trish. She might have been angry that he rejected her advances, if he did."

"Wow, I hadn't considered that."

"All I know is I wish my kids weren't mixed up in all of this." Mary shook her head. "I'm worried, Suzie. I know that you probably think I shouldn't be, but I am."

"I'm worried, too." Suzie took her hand. "I have no idea what's going to happen, but I do know that we need to make sure that Cathy and Ben aren't harmed by any of it."

"And Rick." Mary nodded.

"I'm not so sure about Rick." Suzie put her finger to her lips and peeked around the side of the house. The table where Rick and Cathy had been sitting was empty. She caught sight of them further down the beach. When she turned back to

Mary, she frowned. "I think he's hiding things, important things."

"Like what? He seemed nice enough to me."

"You didn't see what I just saw. When he realized he'd have to talk to Kirk, he kind of flipped out. Poor Cathy was trying to calm him down, but it was like a switch had been flipped inside of him. He said he has problems with authority. It seems to me that he's trying to present himself one way, but underneath, he's something completely different."

"I hope that's not the case. We'll have to keep a closer eye on him."

"Yes. In fact I think it would be best if we start our own investigation into the situation."

"You do?"

"Absolutely. We're talking about Ben and Cathy here. Kirk's a good officer, but we can't leave the fate of your kids in his hands. We need to figure out as soon as possible who did this, so that the three of you can refocus on enjoying your time together."

"I love that we think alike." Mary grinned. "But where are we going to start?"

"I'm not sure yet. Curtis' room and the dive shack are going to be off limits while the crime scene investigators go through them. So I think we should start with the few things that we do know about him."

"He loved going to the library." Mary shrugged. "He spent a lot of time there."

"Yes, he did. Which means that Louis probably has a good idea of what he was up to. We also know at least one person from his past, Jim, who we might be able to get more information from. Then there's Hal and Trish. If we can figure out whether Hal had access to Curtis' equipment we might have a better chance of determining whether he is the killer."

"What strikes me as odd about that, is if Hal was jealous, wouldn't he just confront Curtis?

Maybe lose his temper? Whoever did this, had to put some serious thought into it, and plan to tamper with the equipment. Right?"

"That's true. I guess Hal might have tried to make it look like an accident. But it was clear to Kirk that it probably wasn't, because of Curtis' experience. So, if he did try to make it look like an accident he didn't do a very good job."

"No, that's for sure. I say, let's go down to the library and talk to Louis. We can do some research on Hal, Trish, and Jim while we're there."

"Don't forget Rick." Suzie wagged her finger. "I don't trust him, not even a little bit."

"We can't leave Dune House unguarded though. I'd feel more comfortable if one of us stayed here."

"Yes, you're right. You stay, try to find out what the crime scene techs might have discovered in their search. Keep an eye on everyone. I'll head to the library. That will give you some time with the kids, even if things are tense. I saw Rick and Cathy head down to the beach."

"Okay, I guess I need to think about getting dinner ready, too. I don't think anyone ate lunch."

"Yes, they'll probably be very hungry."

"Text me as soon as you know anything."

"I will."

As Suzie drove away from Dune House she tried not to think about how worried Mary looked. As much as she loved Ben and Cathy, they weren't her kids. They were Mary's, which meant she had to be far more worried than Suzie. Suzie was worried enough to buy them both a plane ticket. However, she knew better than that. The best defense, was finding the real killer.

Chapter Nine

Suzie pulled into the parking lot of the library and parked near the front. When she stepped inside there was a small line at the desk. Louis skimmed a stack of books through the scanner one by one. Suzie checked her watch and realized it was a little after three. That was prime time for the school kids to gather at the library. If she didn't get a chance to talk to Louis now, she might miss it altogether. She waited at the back of the line. Louis looked over the top of his glasses and smiled at her from behind the desk, then turned his focus back on the person he was helping. It wasn't long before Suzie was right in front of him.

"Suzie, is it true?" He stared at her, his smile gone.

"What?"

"Curtis, is he dead?"

"Word travels so fast around here. Yes, I'm

afraid he is, Louis. I'm sorry. I know that you two had become close."

"I wouldn't exactly say that. I was about to start charging him rent for living here."

"He was here that often?"

"Every day for at least a few hours."

"What did he do?"

"Used the computers mostly. He never checked out a book. He would pull some off the shelf, then leave them on the table for me to re-shelve."

"Do you remember what he was looking at?"

"What's going on, I thought it was an accident?"

"Not according to Kirk."

"Interesting. Well, he was mostly looking at books about ancient artifacts, shipwrecks, tombs, that kind of thing."

"Did he mention why he was looking at those

books?"

"I assumed he was trying to find treasure. He asked me once if I knew about an underwater cave that was rumored to be a few miles off the coast, near Bucky's Inlet. I told him that there were lots of rumors about the area, but that was all they were, rumors. He even went so far as to ask me if there were any maps that showed the cave. I told him there was no cave that I knew about, and to please stop bothering me."

"Oh, classic Louis." She smiled.

"Okay, I was a little nicer than that. But he made a lot of extra work for me. Of course I am sad that he's dead. He seemed like a good person, just nervous."

"Nervous? I always thought he was pretty relaxed."

"When he was here, he seemed pretty anxious. He'd check his phone a lot, look at the door, pace, then hunt down another book. It seemed to me that he couldn't settle down."

"That's interesting. It's like we knew two different people. Did you ever take a lesson with him?"

"Oh no, my feet are meant to be on the ground. When it comes to going underwater, I only go up to my chin," Louis said.

"I understand that." She offered a short laugh. "I think some people are just a little too adventurous."

"And yet, here you are, sticking your nose into a murder." He clucked his tongue.

"Is it that obvious?" Suzie raised an eyebrow.

"Yes, to me it is."

"You always can see right through me. Anything you can do to help me out?"

"I'll tell you what I can do, though it needs to stay between us," Louis said.

"Of course it will."

"I can give you access to his history. It'll show all of his internet searches, and also whatever

128

books he searched for. Like I said he never checked any out, so I don't have any record of that, but he did look them up pretty frequently. That should give you some idea of what he might have been looking for."

"Thanks Louis, that would be great."

"Go take that first computer on the left, and I'll open up the history for you."

As Suzie settled in front of the computer she felt a little uneasy. Digging into Curtis' business seemed to be intrusive, but at the same time she was certain that he would want her to figure out who killed him. She took a deep breath and began to look through the search history. She found that he navigated to several websites that offered to sell antiques and other valuable items. She could tell that he'd looked through some of the listings, however she didn't see any posts made by him.

When Suzie began to sort through some of the library catalog searches he'd made, she discovered that he'd been looking up books about valuing antiques, restoration, and the legalities involved in finding foreign treasure. It occurred to her that he might have been planning for another treasure hunt. As interesting as the information was, it didn't really give her a direction to go in. She returned to his internet history and found that he'd looked up the name Jim Smithsy. So Curtis had been looking for his friend Jim before he showed up? She thought that was a little strange.

Then Suzie noticed that Curtis had visited a website that allowed people to search coordinates over water. After some skimming she realized she wasn't going to be able to find the exact coordinates he'd searched. She reached for a slip of paper beside the computer to jot down the website. As she began to write she noticed that the paper had some indentations, as if someone had written on another slip of paper on top of it. She brushed the tiny pencil across the ridges and dips in the paper and soon revealed a set of coordinates. Her heart skipped a beat as she guessed that Curtis had grabbed two slips of paper and realized it after he wrote down the coordinates, then put one back. She typed the coordinates into the website's search engine, and found herself staring at wide open ocean. It told her absolutely nothing.

Maybe Suzie couldn't figure out from the website exactly what the coordinates meant, but she was sure that Paul would be able to help her. He was supposed to dock that evening, and she couldn't wait for him to get there. She was sure he would be able to help her at least figure out what Curtis might have been looking for out on the water. She tucked the paper into her purse. Then she shifted gears. She needed to know more about the people who were under her roof.

As she began to dig through Hal and Trish's background it didn't take her long to find out that Hal had a checkered past. He had a history of assault, and had been arrested at least twice before. Trish on the other hand appeared to be a saint. She worked with many charities, and had a beautiful singing voice, according to a few videos she found on the internet. With Hal's history, it was pretty easy to assume that he could be responsible for Curtis' death. However, the stumbling block was, whether he had the knowledge to contaminate Curtis' equipment.

Suzie began to search for information about Curtis' friend, Jim. He was much harder to pin down. However, using the information from the adventure school where they both took classes she was able to track down some of his social media posts. The most important was a photograph with Curtis, as they celebrated the find of a shipwreck. The post was from a few months ago, and didn't say much about the find itself, but it did claim that both Curtis and Jim found the shipwreck together. She took a snap of it on her phone, and dug a little deeper.

No red flags were raised when she looked at Jim's profile. She couldn't find any family members listed and unlike Curtis he didn't seem to have very many friends, but besides that everything looked pretty normal. Frustrated with the dead ends, she decided to take a break and zero in on Rick. Searching for information on Rick made her feel uneasy. She knew she was invading both Rick's privacy, and Cathy's. It was easy to find information about Rick by navigating through Cathy's social media. She did discover that his parents were deceased. His stint in the navy hadn't lasted long, and though there was no mention of dishonorable discharge, there did seem to be some controversy about why he parted ways with the navy. She also found several pictures of him in diving gear, at different exotic locations. The pictures were dated at least a year before he began dating Cathy. It seemed to her that he was quite an accomplished diver. He would certainly have the knowledge to contaminate Curtis' equipment. But why would he? After reaching another dead end on information about his past, she decided that she was done with her search. The library was packed with kids and parents.

Suzie waved to Louis on her way out the door, but he was occupied with a very long line. On the drive back to Dune House she considered whether Curtis might have been trying to find something in particular. She recalled Louis mentioning the rumor of a nearby underwater cave. Maybe Curtis suspected there was treasure there. She decided to try to find out if the cave actually existed. She parked in front of Dune House and sat in the car for a moment. On the porch she could see the furniture she stained. Just that morning, getting that project done, was the most important thing to her. Now that it was done, she couldn't care less about it. All she wanted to know was what happened to Curtis.

Chapter Ten

Mary glanced at the clock. There was still an hour before she could get started on dinner. She found it difficult to keep herself occupied. Her mind kept turning back to Curtis, and her kids being on the suspect list.

"Mom, have you seen my shoes?" Ben frowned as he walked into the kitchen. "I left them by my bed, and now I can't seem to find them anywhere."

"I haven't seen them. Are you sure you didn't wear them down to the beach at some point?"

"No, I didn't. Maybe Rick took them."

"Why would Rick steal your shoes?"

"I don't think he would steal them, but maybe he wasn't paying attention and took them by mistake. We have the same size foot."

"Hey Ben, how well do you know Rick?"

"Pretty well, I guess. He's always pushing

Cathy to invite me when they go out somewhere."

"Really? Why do you think that is?"

"He said, he didn't want me to feel left out. I think it drives Cathy crazy. I turn down some invites because I know she wants time with him."

"It seems a little odd that he's so clingy so fast, don't you think?"

"I don't know. He said family is important to him. I think he's been through a lot of hard times to be honest."

"Has he told you about any of them?"

"No, but he implies that he's been alone most of his life. I can't imagine what might have happened to his parents. I don't like to be too nosy."

"I understand that." Mary shook her head. "I don't like to be either. But he is dating your sister."

"I'll keep an eye on him, don't worry."

"Here they come now." Mary tilted her head

towards the kitchen window that overlooked the beach. "You can ask Rick about your shoes."

"Thanks Mom." He went out through the front door to meet them. Mary heard some footsteps on the stairs and turned to see Jim.

"Hi Jim, how are you holding up?"

"I'm still trying to make sense out of all of it, to be honest. Curtis was such a good guy, I can't imagine anyone wanting to hurt him."

"Me neither. But when you two worked together, was there anyone that he had problems with?"

"Never. Curtis was always looking out for people. He even gave free lessons to kids that couldn't afford it. He used his day off to do it. We worked together at an adventure business. It offered abseiling, diving, and a few other sports. He focused mostly on the diving, and I took care of the abseiling. He even convinced me to offer some free lessons. Trust me, I wasn't the generous type at the time. But seeing those kids so happy, it changed me. If it wasn't for Curtis, I never would have experienced that."

"Good friends can do that for you." Mary smiled. "I know, Suzie and I have been friends for decades. I wouldn't be here in this beautiful place if it weren't for her."

"I'm so glad you two have each other." He sighed.

"I'm sorry, Jim. Losing Curtis must be very hard on you. Do you have any family that you might reach out to?"

"No, no family. Curtis didn't have any either. That's something we had in common. We both came up in the foster system, though we didn't know each other then. It was something only he and I could talk about, you know?"

"I imagine so." Her heart ached for Jim. He'd been through so much in his young life already, and now he'd lost a good friend. "If there's anything I can do to help, anything at all, just name it. All right?"

"I think I'm just going to go into town to pick up a few things. I hadn't planned to stay, but it doesn't feel right for me to leave until all of this is settled."

"It's probably best that you don't. Kirk may need more information from you."

"Yes, I know." He shook his head. "I wish I knew something that would help. I'll be back in a little while."

"Dinner's at five."

"I'll be here."

As he headed for the door, Suzie opened it. She nodded to Jim as he stepped past her, then headed straight for Mary.

"How are the kids holding up?"

"Okay, I think. Cathy is attached to Rick's hip, and someone has stolen Ben's shoes."

"Well, I found out a little information at the library." Suzie filled her in on what Curtis' search habits were at the library. She showed Mary the coordinates and explained how she had got them. "I think he was on to something. Maybe he was trying to find that cave. Maybe he was trying to find treasure. Whatever it was, I think he was willing to risk his life to get it, and in the end it did cost him his life."

"So you think someone murdered him because he found treasure?"

"Maybe?" Suzie shrugged. "Or maybe not. I'm not sure. But Paul's meant to dock today so I am going to talk to him tonight about finding that cave. It has to have something to do with all of this."

"But Louis said it was just a rumor, right?"

"Yes, he did, but Louis doesn't know everything"

"Really?"

"He knows almost everything, not everything."

"Don't tell him that." Mary winked. "Let me

know what Paul says. I can handle dinner here. You deserve a night away from all of this. Take him to dinner."

"I think I will do that. I don't want to throw him right into the middle of all of this without having a chance to talk to him first. But are you sure you want to do dinner by yourself? With Trish and Hal?"

"I'm not worried about it. Besides, Cathy and Ben will be here with me. I will be just fine. Stop worrying about me, and find out about that cave."

"Thanks Mary." She headed up the stairs with a particular blouse in mind that she wanted to wear to greet Paul. As she passed Ben and Rick's room, she noticed that the door was open. Her investigative past insisted that she take a look through his things. The desire for Cathy to trust her fought against the urge. She lingered in the doorway for a few more seconds, then took a step inside. She had to check the linens, and things. That was her excuse. She noticed Rick's bag. It was open on the foot of his bed. As she walked towards it, her heart seemed to grow too big to be contained by her chest. She reached for the bag.

"Aunt Suzie?"

She froze, then glanced over her shoulder at Ben. "Hi."

"Hi. What are you doing?"

"Oh, your mother told me that your shoes were missing. I thought I'd take a look around for you."

"Don't worry, I'm sure that they will turn up. I just need flipflops for hanging out on the beach anyway, right?"

"Sure, okay. If I see them, I'll let you know."

"Great, thanks." He smiled.

Suzie excused herself from the room and hurried into her own. As soon as the door was closed she let out a breath of relief. She was lucky it was Ben and not Rick who caught her snooping. After a few moments to calm down, she changed, and headed back down the stairs. The kitchen smelled lovely with whatever Mary was cooking, but there was no one in sight to enjoy it. She caught a glimpse of Cathy, Ben, and Rick on the deck, then spotted Mary near the side door. To her surprise, Mary swung it open, and stepped in.

"Oh wow, did the locksmith come out?"

"Oh yes, I'm sorry, I'm so scatter-brained today. He came out while you were at the library. It's all fixed now."

"Great. That's one good thing I guess."

"We need as many as we can get. Go enjoy your evening with Paul, that's a very good thing."

"Yes, I hope it will be."

Suzie headed towards the dock. When she parked she noticed that Paul's boat was already in the slip. She headed down the wooden planks to meet him. As she approached the boat he emerged from the cabin and smiled at her.

"You are a beautiful sight."

"Thanks." She returned the smile. "So are you."

"Coming on board?" He offered her his hand.

"Yes please." She climbed onto the boat with his hand to steady her. Once on board she hugged him, then shared a lingering kiss.

"Every time I leave, I wonder if I've lost my mind to leave you behind." He gazed into her eyes.

"But isn't it so sweet when we reunite?"

"Yes, it is." He kissed her forehead. "So, what kind of wild adventures did you have while I was gone?"

"Unfortunately, no adventures, only tragedy."

"Tragedy?" He led her into the cabin and pulled out a bottle of wine. "What happened?"

"Curtis was murdered."

"Curtis?" He nearly dropped one of the wine glasses. "How? By who?"

"Someone tampered with his equipment, Kirk

doesn't know who yet."

"That's awful. Does he have any suspects?"

"Just everyone at Dune House." Suzie frowned. "Including Mary's children."

"What? That's ridiculous."

"Yes, it is, but it doesn't change the fact that they are suspects. Mary and I have been trying to get to the bottom of things, but we don't have much to go on."

"This must be rough on both of you." He poured the wine and handed her the glass. "How is Mary holding up?"

"I think she's okay, but she's a nervous wreck. On top of her kids being on the suspect list, Cathy's boyfriend who she brought along is also. Honestly, I don't trust the guy."

"Would you trust anyone that dated Cathy?" He took a sip of his wine.

"Probably not. But this guy has some real issues. He has temper problems, and he's an experienced diver. Something went wrong while he was in the navy. Everything about him just feels off."

"Hm. Your instincts are usually pretty good. Do you think he did this?"

"I'm not sure. The obvious suspect is Hal, remember you met him before you launched?"

"Yes. He seemed like a decent guy."

"He did, I know. But there were some issues between him and Curtis. It's so tough to put my finger on who might have done this. At least I know it wasn't Ben or Cathy."

"That's a relief. Does Kirk know that?"

"I'm not sure. They don't have alibis, so he won't remove them from the suspect list. But he's been polite about it."

"Mary must be beside herself." Paul finished his wine. "I'm sorry you were dealing with this all alone, but I'm here now."

"And I'm so glad." She wrapped her arms

around him and closed her eyes. After a few moments of savoring his warmth, she recalled the question she wanted to ask him. "Do you know anything about a secret underwater cave around here, near Bucky's Inlet?"

"Oh, you've heard about the cave?" He laughed.

"So there is one?"

"No." He shook his head. "That's an old story that some of the teens of my generation made up. It was to keep people away from their island."

"Island? No secret underwater cave, but there is a secret island?"

"It's not really secret, just tiny and unpopular. At least it was. The idea of the cave and its supposed location was to divert attention from the island. Teenagers like to use it for fun and not be interrupted by adults."

"Ah, I see. So you're sure there's no cave?"

"I'm certain. Why?"

"I think Curtis was searching for it before he died. I thought maybe if he found it, it might have something to do with his death."

"No, there's no cave. I'm not sure why he would be looking for it."

"One more dead end." She frowned.

"Hey, try not to worry." He looked into her eyes. "This will all get settled soon enough. It's going to be hard going through it, but Curtis' death will be solved."

"How can you be so confident? Jason isn't here, and there is no real evidence."

"Kirk is very capable and Jason trained Kirk, and as far as evidence, give it time. Things have a strange way of coming to the surface if you're patient."

"I'm just worried about Mary."

"And you?" He brushed his thumb along her cheek. "You're always thinking of others, but I'm sure this has been a struggle for you, too."

"Yes, it has been." She glanced away from him. "I keep thinking, maybe if I'd noticed something, maybe Curtis would still be alive."

"But you know that isn't true. There was nothing that you could have done."

"Maybe not, but it's eerie to think that the murderer might be under my own roof." She sighed, then filled him in on the suspects. "I was certain that it had to be Hal, he has the criminal background, he had motive, and I've seen a bit of his temper. But no matter how I spin it, I can't find enough motive. Sure, he was jealous over Trish, but jealous enough to kill? It took forethought to kill Curtis, not just a boiled over temper."

"Not to worry, that's Kirk's job."

"No, it's mine, and Mary's, because as long as the kids are caught up in this, they are in danger. Honestly, I'm starting to suspect that this has to do with treasure. Do you think it could? Doesn't that sound crazy?"

"Yes, it absolutely could, and no it doesn't sound crazy. Treasure hunters take their adventures very seriously, and they are highly secretive about what they find, and where they find it."

"So if Curtis found something of value, and he was trying to hide it from others, maybe someone came after him for it?"

"It's very possible. Everyone thinks of treasure hunting as just some pipe dream, but if you find a good sunken ship, or some ancient coins, it can make you rich."

"Wow, I didn't realize that was even still a thing."

"It is, and those who are dedicated to finding it, are very passionate about what they do."

"Maybe that's why he asked Cathy about finding more information about some artifacts. Maybe he found something!"

"Even if he did, unless you have an idea of

where it might be it won't make any difference."

His words reminded her of the slip of paper in her pocket. She fished it out and held it out to him.

"Do you have any idea what this might mean? It's the only scrap of evidence that I've found so far."

"Let me take a look." Paul studied it for a moment, then nodded. "It's coordinates."

"I know that, but when I looked them up, it just showed open ocean."

"Well, that makes sense. If he was a treasure hunter, then it's probably a dive site."

"Yes, that does make sense. So he used these coordinates to find the site?"

"Yes. It's difficult to pinpoint the exact location of a shipwreck, but if you can get close, then you can usually find it."

"I found a picture of Jim and Curtis celebrating the find of a shipwreck. I wonder if it might be the same one."

"If it is, then Jim should know all about it."

"But he hasn't mentioned it. At least, I don't think he has. He said something to Curtis at dinner about dangerous dives and I did see a photo on the internet of them celebrating the find of a shipwreck together."

"Let me check something." He entered the coordinates into a device, then nodded. "Yes, this would be a very dangerous area to dive in. The currents are strong, and pretty frequent sightings of sharks. Only experts would risk diving in this area, and even they would be hesitant."

"So Curtis took a huge risk if he went diving here, with Jim, and found the shipwreck."

"Yes."

"Then he must have had some strong motivation."

"I'd say so." Paul shook his head. "I don't know exactly what he was up to, but I'd say that there might be a lot more to this murder than you realize."

"Jim might be the only one who knows the truth. Maybe he knew enough that he wanted to kill Curtis."

"Maybe. But you said they're good friends, didn't you?"

"They are, but friendship doesn't always last. Curtis was doing searches on Jim before he died. Maybe they lost contact, and Curtis was trying to reach him for some reason. But, Curtis was surprised, or at least seemed that way, when Jim showed up at Dune House. He wasn't expecting him."

"Interesting. So, if Curtis wasn't looking for Jim to contact him, maybe he was looking for him to figure out where he was."

"Maybe. Also how did Jim leave Dune House without me or Mary noticing, the lock on the side door was jammed so we couldn't open it and I was on the porch and Mary was out back. We would have seen him."

"You might have missed him," Paul said.

"Maybe, but I don't see how." Suzie ran her hand across her forehead. "All of this is exhausting."

"Then let's take a break from it. Just for tonight, let's focus on you and me. We can take a fresh look at things in the morning, okay?"

"Yes. That sounds perfect." She kissed his cheek and closed her eyes. As much as she wanted all of her focus to be on him, she knew it wouldn't be, not until she was certain that Ben and Cathy were safe, and Curtis' killer had been found.

Chapter Eleven

Mary finished the dishes from dinner and began to dry them. She could hear Ben, Cathy, and Rick outside on the deck. She tried not to listen in to their conversation, but snippets of it drew her attention.

"I can't believe any of this is happening."

"Don't worry about it too much, Ben. I'm sure that the police will find his killer." Cathy's voice drifted through the kitchen window.

"Unless they're the type that just likes to wrap up a case without actually finding the killer. You know, a cop that picks someone who looks guilty enough to pass, and just throws the cuffs on." Rick's voice had a nervous tremble in it.

"Rick, stop. You're going to scare Ben," Cathy said.

"I'm not a child, you know. I'm aware of how the world works. But I don't think Kirk is like that.

Mom and Suzie are friends with him. I'm sure that he's a stand-up guy," Ben said.

"I bet you're right. Mom is usually a good judge of character. if she trusts Kirk then I think we can trust him, too."

Mary's heart sank. She wanted her children to be able to trust her judgment. But could they? Could she trust Kirk? An image of both of them being led away in handcuffs flashed through her mind. It was almost impossible not to be overwhelmed by the thought of it. Tears stung her eyes as panic grew within her. Hopefully Suzie would find out something about the underwater cave. She finished the dishes, then walked into the living room. A sound from the couch startled her.

"Trish, I didn't even know you were there."

"I'm sorry." She sniffled. "I needed some space from Hal."

"Are you okay?" Mary sat down on the couch beside her. "Do you want to talk about it?"

"I don't know what to say. I feel like I caused this whole problem. If it wasn't for me being silly with Curtis, the police wouldn't even be looking at Hal as a suspect."

"The police are looking at all of us as suspects. They have to, until they find the killer. None of this is your fault."

"I keep trying to tell myself that, but I'm not sure if I believe it."

"This is a hard time for all of us. But I can assure you that Kirk will do a fantastic job of investigating the case."

"Thank you. That does make me feel a little better." Trish smiled slightly. "Hal's gone down to the beach with the key to our room, do you have a second key for me?"

"Sure, I'll get it for you." Mary walked back over to the desk and noticed that Jim's paperwork was still not filled out. She retrieved a key for Trish and gave it to her. As she turned back, Jim walked through the hall.

"Jim!"

"Yes?" He stopped and looked at her.

"I missed you at dinner."

"Sorry, I'm having a hard time being social right now."

"I understand. Did you have something to eat?"

"Yes, I grabbed something in town."

"Listen, I hate to bother you, but I really do need to fill in your information for our records."

"I understand. What do you need?"

"Just an address and driver's license number."

"This should do then." He reached into his wallet and pulled out his driver's license. As he handed it over to Mary, a piece of paper fell to the floor that must have been tucked behind it. She reached for it to hand it back to him, but he was already up the stairs. When she picked up the piece of paper and started to fold it back up, her eyes widened. It was the same set of numbers that Suzie found at the library. The paper seemed too worn to be new. She reached for her phone to call Suzie, but the front door swung open before she could.

"Hi Mary."

"Home so early?"

"Paul was tired, and I didn't want you to be alone here too long."

"Look what I found." Mary held out the slip of paper. "It fell out of Jim's wallet."

"Oh wow, that's the same coordinates. It looks like both Jim and Curtis were at that location at some point, most likely together."

"I'm going to make a copy of his driver's license." Mary carried it behind the desk. "He's upstairs in his room."

"I'm going to go talk to him. I'll take his license back to him," Suzie said.

"Do you really think that's a good idea?"

"I want to get a better grasp on him, and who he is. He's our only real connection to Curtis."

"All right, do you want me to come with you?"

"No, I don't want him to feel ambushed. I'll let you know what I find out."

"Okay. Here." Mary handed her the driver's license. "I'm done with this."

"Thanks." Suzie grabbed the license and headed up the stairs. After having some time with Paul she felt more centered. No matter what, the murder had to be solved. When she reached the third floor she knocked on the door.

"Can I help you?" Jim asked as he opened the door.

"Your driver's license." Suzie smiled as she offered it to him.

"Thanks." He took it and started to close the door. She wedged her foot in before he could close it.

"Could I talk to you for a moment, please?"

"I guess." He swung the door back open. She glanced past him at the room. Everything was just as she'd left it.

"You mentioned something at dinner, about a dangerous dive that you and Curtis went on. I was just curious, and this might sound very silly, but did you and Curtis ever go on other dives more recently and find some kind of treasure?"

"Excuse me?" He narrowed his eyes. "Why are you asking me this?"

"Honestly, I'm just curious. I didn't think there were any real treasure hunters left in the world. I guess it's a part of Curtis that I didn't have the chance to know."

"Yes, Curtis was a hunter, so was I. We were partners for a long time."

"Did you ever find anything recently?"

"Uh, just some old shipwreck."

"Well, that must have been exciting."

"Not really. It was already picked bare when

we found it. Nothing much to it."

"Still, finding it must have been…"

"Finding an old shipwreck that someone else has already found is not exciting. It's disappointing. Curtis and I invested all of our money in that dive, and we lost it all."

"I'm sorry about that."

"Me too. Now, if you don't mind, I'd like to turn in."

"All right. Do you need any fresh linens?"

"No, thanks I'm fine."

"What about a clean? I can do a quick tidy."

"No, thank you. I prefer my privacy."

"Okay, I understand. If there's anything you need, just let me know."

"Thanks, I will." He closed the door and she heard the lock engage. For a moment she lingered in the hallway. She really wanted to have a look around his room, but while he was in it, she knew that wouldn't be possible. At least he had confirmed that he'd found a shipwreck with Curtis. But if they'd both lost everything on the dive, and there was no treasure to recover, what motive would Jim have to kill him?

When Suzie met Mary downstairs again, she shared with her the information she'd found, and also what Paul told her about the cave and the island.

"So why was Curtis looking for the cave?"

"I would guess to hide something there. Or maybe he thought something was already hidden there."

"The treasure from the shipwreck?" Mary raised an eyebrow.

"I don't know. Jim said there wasn't anything at the shipwreck. Why would he lie about it?"

"I'm not sure. Maybe Curtis found something on a different dive."

"Maybe." Suzie sighed. "I'm going to bed. I'm

exhausted."

"Me too. Hal and Trish are in their rooms, I saw Ben go up a little while ago. I have no idea where Cathy and Rick are, but I'm sure they'll be back soon."

"I'll see you in the morning, Mary."

"Yes. Try to get some sleep, Suzie."

Chapter Twelve

Mary didn't close her eyes until she heard the front door open and Cathy's voice. Once she knew she was home, she was able to close her eyes and begin to fall asleep. It had been the same way since they were born. She needed to know that her kids were safe in bed before she could go to sleep herself. Once she was asleep, her dreams tormented her. Curtis on the beach, Curtis at the breakfast table, Curtis with his wide smile and eagerness to help with whatever task she couldn't manage. When she woke the next morning she could barely comprehend the idea that he was dead. It took her a few minutes before all of the events filtered back through her mind. With a heavy heart she made her way into the kitchen to start the coffee. She'd barely gotten a pot brewed when there was a knock on the front door. It was just after seven, quite early for anyone to pay a visit. Before she could get the door, Suzie opened it. Only then did Mary realize that Suzie was already up.

"I guess she didn't sleep well either," Mary said to herself and frowned. She headed back to her room to change into something other than pajamas. From the front door she heard Suzie's voice.

"Kirk, good morning. Did you find something?"

"No unfortunately, not yet. That's why I'm here. I wanted to start my morning off with the only lead I have. That's right here, at Dune House."

"Well, you're welcome to come in, I'm not sure what else we have to share with you, but of course we are happy to help. There's some fresh coffee."

"Great, I could use some."

Suzie smiled as she led him to the kitchen. She guessed he might have come to Dune House just to get a cup of coffee. She set out three mugs, then poured one for Kirk. "Anything in it?"

"Information?" He smiled.

"I've told you everything I know, Kirk."

"Well, I need to know more. Maybe there's something that you didn't notice. Something that you saw, but you didn't understand was important."

"I'm a pretty observant person."

"All the more reason to pick your brain."

"Lovely." She quirked a brow and poured her own mug of coffee, then poured one for Mary as well.

"Cathy, Ben, and Rick are here from out of town. We can't ignore that they might have some kind of involvement in this crime."

"There's no way that Cathy or Ben had anything to do with it."

"Rick?"

"Honestly, I don't know much about him, but I doubt it. Cathy is a good judge of character, like her mother."

"What about Ben?"

"What about him?"

"He seemed very nervous when I spoke with him."

"He's barely an adult."

Kirk set his mug back down on the counter and turned to face her.

"Why do I get the feeling that you're not telling me everything, Suzie?"

"I don't know." She picked up the mug and turned on the tap to wash it.

"The only way for me to do my job is if I can rely on my witnesses to be honest with me."

"I am not a witness." She turned off the water and set the glass in the drainer. "I didn't see Curtis die."

"No, you didn't. But you saw him day in and day out. You saw most of my suspect pool, far more than I did. You're a great source of information to me. I just don't understand why you wouldn't want to help me. Unless you're protecting someone?"

"Kirk, you're imagining things."

"Am I?" He frowned. "I have a feeling if Jason was here you'd be much more cooperative." He tried to meet her eyes. "Maybe you haven't known me long enough to trust me, but my only goal is to find the murderer. If you have information that can help with that, you should tell me."

"If I had information that would help with that, I would tell you. Maybe you haven't known me long enough to know that you can trust me, Kirk. I would never hinder an investigation."

"But you are." He crossed his arms. "I can tell that you're hiding something from me. Anytime I bring up Ben, you avoid the subject. You skirt around any personal information about him as if you've never even met him before. I know that you're very close to him, have been part of his life since he was a child. So I'm not buying the amnesia."

"It's not amnesia."

"Then tell me the truth." He shook his head. "Whatever you are trying to hide, I'm going to find out about it. It may take me a few more days, but I'm going to get to the truth. It would be better if it came from you, wouldn't it? So that you can explain whatever it is that you're hiding?"

Suzie closed her eyes. She didn't want to do anything to put Ben in danger, but she did know that with a little digging he would be able to find out about Ben's financial troubles.

"He had nothing to do with this, Kirk."

"Then let me prove that. Let me clear his name. I can't do that unless I have accurate information."

"You're going to have to talk to Mary."

"Does Mary know everything that you do?"

"Do I?" Mary stepped into the kitchen and looked between the two. "What are we talking about here?"

"Ben." Suzie frowned. "I'm sorry, Mary."

"Don't be. It's okay. He hasn't done anything wrong."

"Then why are you two dodging my questions about him?" He rested his hands on his hips.

"It's not what you think." Mary sighed. "My son has gotten himself into some trouble, and he asked me not to bring the police into it. It has nothing to do with any of this."

"I need to be the judge of that. So please, share it with me."

"She doesn't have to…"

"No, Suzie it's fine. Kirk's right, we should be cooperating in every way we can. We all have the same goal. Ben took a loan from a loan shark, and the guy has been harassing him. That's all."

"He got tangled up with a loan shark? That's not a good idea."

"No, it isn't, but it's a mess he got himself into, and we are going to handle it."

"How are you going to do that?" Kirk shifted from one foot to the other. "These people are not the type that you want to play around with. They can be very vengeful, and violent."

"I'm aware, Kirk."

"So? Let me look into this guy for you."

"My son would rather we didn't go to the police about this. I thought maybe Jason…"

"Look, I know Jason is like family to you as well. I get that. But I am here to help you also. As far as this investigation goes, I need to know that you are going to be forthcoming from now on. I take a murder on my beach very seriously, and I'm not going to wait until Jason gets back to solve it. All right?"

"All right." Suzie nodded as she stared at him.

Kirk had more backbone than she expected, and she admired him for it. "Anything we come across, we'll do our best to keep you informed."

"Good." He shifted his gaze between them, then nodded. "When you're ready to talk about what we can do to help your son, you let me know."

"I will." Mary cleared her throat. "Thank you, Kirk. I really appreciate the offer."

"And I appreciate your honesty." As he turned to leave, Suzie was tempted to remind him that Ben had nothing to do with the murder, however Mary beat her to it.

"No matter what happens, Kirk, keep in mind, Ben is not a suspect here."

Kirk paused at the door and looked back over his shoulder at her. "He's not a suspect in your eyes. But in my eyes, until I've found the killer, every single person who had contact with Curtis in the hours before his death, is a suspect." He stepped out without another word and closed the door behind him. Mary reached for Suzie's hand and sighed.

"Don't worry, Mary. Ben will be fine."

"I hope so. But my instincts are telling me something different. We need to figure out why Curtis was killed, and fast. That might give us some idea about who did it."

"Then I need to go to the one place he looked into when he was here."

"What do you mean?"

"The coordinates that Jim and Curtis both have, maybe they went diving there, maybe that was where the shipwreck was. It is a couple of hours away, but I can hire some divers to check things out. If I leave after breakfast today I can be back in time for lunch."

"All right, but I'm going with you."

"But Mary you aren't exactly fond of boats."

"I'll be fine, I'm not letting you go without me. What do you think we're going to find?"

"I'm not sure, but it's an opportunity to retrace Curtis' steps. I'll meet you down at the docks after breakfast."

"Are you going to have Paul take us out?"

"No, he needs his rest, he has to go on a few more short trips this week, he's showing a new fisherman to the area the ropes. The divers should have a boat."

"Okay, I'll meet you there."

Chapter Thirteen

About an hour later Suzie and Mary were on the deck of an unfamiliar boat, headed far out into the wide-open ocean.

"Suzie, maybe we should have waited until Paul was free and brought him along." Mary clung to the railing and tried not to think about how far away from land they were.

"I didn't want to bother him and we might not find anything at all, then we would have wasted Paul's time."

"I think you're just afraid to admit that you wanted to go on a treasure hunt."

"What's so wrong with that?" Suzie's eyes widened. "If we were to find any real treasure, it would be pretty amazing, wouldn't it?"

"Yes, it would, but it's unlikely. I'm betting that all Curtis left out here was some empty boxes. Even if he had hidden treasure somewhere, whoever killed him most likely has it. If he was killed for it, then they wouldn't have let things get too far without finding out where the treasure was."

"Maybe that's true. But I'm willing to look anyway. It's the only lead that we have right now."

"You mean, other than Hal?" Mary tapped her fingernails against the railing of the ship. "I think that we can both agree Hal is still the main suspect here."

"I do agree. But until we find out more about what Curtis was trying to find, we're not going to have any solid evidence either way. If we retrace his steps we might just be able to get this case solved in time for you to get some quality time with your kids."

"I still don't know what I'm going to do about Ben." She shook her head. "I can't believe he got himself into this mess. I swear, I taught him better than this."

"I'm sure you did, but you can remember

what it was like to be his age. It's so easy to think that you have everything figured out, it takes years before you realize that you don't actually have a clue."

"I know, I know, but this is a big mistake. It could affect him for the rest of his life."

"We're not going to let it get that far." Suzie patted her shoulder. "We're going to make sure that this guy gets stopped in his tracks."

When the boat slowed, Suzie's heart sped up. This was it. This was the moment when they would find out if the shipwreck was actually there, and potentially the treasure right along with it. The captain stayed onboard as the two divers they hired launched off into the water.

"Do you think they'll find anything?" Mary clutched Suzie's hand.

"I don't know, I hope so." Suzie frowned. "We need some kind of direction in this case."

After some time, the divers surfaced and

climbed back onto the boat.

"There is definitely a shipwreck down there, a huge one." The first diver began to remove his equipment.

"We took a swim through but there was no sign of any valuables." The second diver sat down beside him. "We can't look any further. The structure of the ship isn't sound, and the currents are too strong, I'm sorry."

"That's all right." Suzie smiled. "At least we know we're getting somewhere now."

"The question is where? Just because Jim and Curtis found a shipwreck, that doesn't mean that Curtis was murdered over it. If there was nothing there to find, then why would Curtis be killed?"

"Maybe there was something there. Maybe Jim killed Curtis for it. Or maybe Curtis took it, or maybe someone thinks that Curtis did."

"Like Jim?"

"Jim was there with him, so it would seem

strange if he thought Curtis found something. But maybe someone in their circle, like Rick."

"How would Rick be in their circle?"

"He's a diver. Maybe they crossed paths at some point."

"Maybe." Mary frowned.

When they made it back to Dune House, Kirk was there to greet them.

"You ladies have been hard to track down today."

"Did you need us for something?" Mary sat down in one of the rocking chairs on the front porch.

"I did. We finished the search of the dive shack. I was wondering if either of you recognize these shoes." He held up a plastic evidence bag with a bright pair of green and gold sneakers inside.

"No." Suzie shook her head. "All I ever saw Curtis in was flipflops."

"Yes, or very rarely sandals. I don't think he owned a pair of socks." Mary shook her head.

"Then these shoes may belong to the killer, they aren't Curtis' shoe size. Whoever it is, is probably missing them. Please let me know if anyone mentions anything about them." As he turned and walked away Mary's heart flipped. She recalled Ben looking for his shoes. She hadn't noticed what his shoes looked like when he arrived. She couldn't be sure that the shoes Kirk had were Ben's. But it was strange that Ben was missing shoes, when shoes had been found in the dive shack. She bit into her bottom lip as she wondered if Suzie would remember that Ben's shoes were missing. If she did, she didn't mention it.

"I'm going to visit Paul for a little bit. Maybe he can give me some direction on where to go next."

"All right, I'll take care of lunch and check in with the guests." As soon as Suzie left, Mary grabbed her cell phone and sent a text to Ben.

Did you find your shoes yet?

Her hand trembled as she waited for the response. After a few minutes, she received one.

Not yet. Rick said he didn't take them. I don't know who did, but they are gone. It's really strange.

She stared at the text on her phone. The last thing she wanted to do was accuse her son of anything criminal, but how did his sneakers end up in the dive shack? He would have worn flipflops to go to the lesson. Maybe they weren't his shoes at all. Maybe she was jumping to conclusions.

Mary set about preparing lunch. When Ben walked in, she pulled him to the side.

"Ben, what did your shoes look like?"

"Green, with gold stripes. Real bright."

"I think someone found them." Her shoulders slumped as his description matched the shoes that Kirk had found.

"Oh, great."

Mary glanced over her shoulder to make sure that no one was nearby to hear her, then she lowered her voice.

"I think that Kirk found them in the dive shack. Why would they be there?"

"What?" Ben's eyes widened. "They wouldn't be. I haven't even worn them since I got here. I swear, Mom."

"I believe you, Ben, but you're going to have to tell Kirk that the shoes he found are most likely yours."

"Mom, if I do that he's going to suspect me."

"Yes, he might, but he'll suspect you more if he finds out on his own. You have to tell the truth. If you don't, I will."

"Mom, seriously. You can't do this. You know I had nothing to do with this." He stared into her eyes.

"I know that you didn't, Ben, but that doesn't matter. We can't hide this from Kirk. I didn't tell him they were yours, because I wasn't sure. But now that I know, we have to tell him."

"Mom, please. This is only going to make things worse. At least give me until tomorrow. Maybe I can find out why they were there."

"I'll give you until the next time I speak to Kirk, but that's as much as I can give you. Even that isn't right. I love you, Ben, more than I can ever say, but part of being your mother is showing you there is a right way to do things, and a wrong way. Withholding information in an investigation is not the right way."

"I know, Mom." He shook his head. "But there has to be some kind of explanation. I just need a little time to find it."

"All right, Ben, do what you can. But be careful. Whoever did this, may have been trying to frame you by putting your shoes in the shack. Don't you think it could have been Rick?"

"Rick?" Ben drew a sharp breath. "I didn't even consider that."

"You two are sharing a room. You thought he took your shoes in the first place."

"Yes, I did. But I mean, it's Rick."

"I'm giving you a new room tonight. I don't want you sleeping in his room."

"We should leave things as they are. Maybe he'll reveal something if we don't throw up any red flags," Ben suggested.

"Ben, this is your safety we're talking about."

"Rick has no reason to do anything to me, as long as he doesn't think I suspect him. If I change rooms now, he'll suspect that we suspect. Besides, if I'm in his room, I can keep an eye on him. I'll make sure he doesn't go off alone with Cathy."

"All right. Fine for now, but be careful. Understand me?"

"I do." He nodded. "I'll let you know if anything comes up."

"Thanks. Now let's eat lunch."

"Good, I'm starving."

Mary watched her son head for the table. As Rick walked in with Cathy at his side, her heart fluttered. Just how much danger were her children in?

Chapter Fourteen

Suzie knocked on Paul's door. He opened it and smiled as she stepped inside.

"How are you doing?"

"Confused, honestly."

"About the murder?"

"Yes."

"We found it." She pushed the door closed behind her.

"You found what?"

"The shipwreck."

"Are you serious?" He stared into her eyes.

"Yes, I mean, I didn't see it with my own eyes, but the divers I hired confirmed it. They couldn't stay down long, but the shipwreck is definitely there."

"Are you going to tell Kirk about it?"

"I think so." She frowned.

"I thought you said you were going to cooperate with the investigation?"

"Of course I am. This isn't about hiding anything from him. The moment I tell him where the shipwreck is, the murderer might find out and then it might make them panic and hide any evidence or even make them go into hiding."

"You might have to risk that. If you don't you might be the one at risk?" He shook his head. "You're getting too deep into this. You now know where the shipwreck is, that makes you vulnerable."

"It's not as if we found the treasure."

"No, maybe not, but Curtis' killer doesn't know that. If he or she gets wind of you being at the shipwreck, then you might be at risk. You've put yourself in a very vulnerable position here, so what are you going to do to get out of it?"

"I'm not sure yet. I guess I hoped finding the shipwreck would give us some idea of who might have done this. But to be honest we don't even

188

know if the shipwreck has anything to do with the murder. The murderer could be Hal, it could be Trish, it could be Jim, it could even be Rick. I'm no closer to figuring out who it is."

"Could it be someone else entirely? Someone from town, or someone that Curtis interacted with that we didn't know about?"

"It could be, but I don't think so. I really don't. He didn't know many people, and he wasn't here for that long. My instincts tell me that the people that surrounded him in his last days are the people to look at. I definitely think that's the best place to look, at least at the moment."

"Doesn't that include Cathy and Ben?"

"For Kirk it does. But I know they had nothing to do with any of it. Mary and I have to make sure that Kirk knows that, too."

"Whatever I can do to help, just tell me."

"You already are, just by listening."

"Return the favor, and listen to what I'm

saying. When it comes to riches, great men become evil. Please be careful, Suzie."

"I will be." She smiled and kissed his cheek. He turned his head and coaxed her into a passionate kiss. When the kiss broke, Suzie looked into his eyes. "What if Jim lied about there being no treasure?"

"What do you mean?"

"I mean, what if he lied, and conned his friend out of the goods? What if there was treasure and Jim killed Curtis so he could keep it for himself?"

"I guess that's possible. And if he did, then Jim would be a very good suspect."

"Or maybe Curtis lied to Jim about there being no treasure and Jim found out."

"Maybe. But you said they were friendly. Why would Jim be friendly to him if he believed that Curtis stole the treasure out from under his nose?"

"Maybe because Jim didn't want Curtis to

know that he knew or that he was about to run off with the treasure. Maybe that's why Curtis was so surprised when Jim showed up. All I know is that if Curtis did take the treasure, then he had to put it somewhere. If that's the case that might be why he was looking for that cave," Suzie said.

"Oh yes, that makes sense. He was looking for a place to hide it. But the cave doesn't exist."

"Yes, you're right. It's just another dead end."

"Why don't you and I get some lunch and just enjoy our time together?" Paul asked. "Taking your mind off things might loosen up some new ideas."

"That sounds good to me."

***

Suzie returned to Dune House after lunch, to find it empty, but for Mary, who was finishing up the lunch dishes.

"Mary, how did lunch go?"

"Hal and Trish weren't here for it, neither was

Jim. Just the kids and Rick." Her voice shuddered as she spoke his name.

"What's going on? Did you find out something?"

Mary filled her in about Ben's missing shoes, and blushed as she looked into Suzie's eyes. "Do you think I'm wrong for keeping it from Kirk?"

"No, I don't. We both know it wasn't Ben that put those sneakers in the dive shack. I thought of something while I was with Paul. What if Jim and Curtis found the treasure and Jim killed Curtis for it? Or maybe Curtis lied about finding the treasure? What if he found it, and hid it somewhere? Maybe someone is trying to find it."

"Oh, that would be a very strong motive for murder."

"Yes, it would."

"But how can we know if he found anything?"

"Maybe the divers we hired will know something. They're experienced with these kinds of things. I'm going to give them a call."

"Okay. Now is a good time, there's no one else in the house."

"I'm calling now." Suzie sat down at the dining room table and dialed the number for Joe, one of the divers. When Joe answered she held her breath for a moment. He might tell her she was crazy for asking. "Joe, I was wondering. Do you think it's possible that there was treasure on that shipwreck?"

"I'm sure there was at one point, I did some research on the ship and it's a high-end ship known to have transported large amounts of wealth, but it's not there now."

"So someone took it?"

"It looks that way. There's nothing reported on the registry of finds either. I checked when we got back. So whoever took it, kept it to themselves. Any finds are supposed to be reported. If the shipwreck is foreign, it's possible for the country it belonged to, to have a claim to it. Without reporting it, it's hard to sell anything that's found."

"When I hired you, you said you would have to file paperwork to dive. Does everyone have to do that?"

"It's a safety measure and it is highly recommended. Some people don't file the paperwork, but most do. If you dive in a dangerous location without filing you can be at risk of losing your license."

"Thanks Joe."

"I'm sorry we didn't find what you were looking for."

"That's all right. I appreciate your hard work." She hung up the phone and looked into Mary's eyes. "There was most likely treasure there once, someone took it."

"Curtis?"

"It's the only lead we have. I think there is a way we can find out. I need to make a few calls.

You and the kids go out today, get away from all of this. When you come home, we'll check in about the case."

"Suzie, how can I relax and have a good time with them when I know at any moment Kirk might pull up and arrest Ben?"

"Don't worry about Kirk. He's on our side. Just enjoy your time with your kids."

"I'll try. But with Rick being a suspect it's hard."

"I know it is. Maybe he'll let something slip while you're out and relaxing."

"That's a good idea. I didn't think of that."

"Don't worry, if anything big happens, I'll let you know."

"Okay, thanks Suzie."

As Mary walked away, Suzie began to search on her phone. Once she found the right number to call, she placed the call. She used some of her skills that she had learned as an investigative journalist and about thirty minutes later she had access to online records of all of the dives in the area of the shipwreck, including the dates, and the divers. It was a tedious process, but once she narrowed down the dates she was able to come up with a list of names. Right away she noticed that Curtis' name was on the list, twice, about two weeks apart. The first date was a week before he checked in at Dune House, the second was a week after. So he'd visited the shipwreck area at least twice. Did he manage to locate the shipwreck on the first visit? Did he go back to retrieve the treasure?

It was hard to decipher what his purpose was without more information. She skimmed the list a little further. When she noticed one name in particular, her heart lurched. R. Norris. Norris was a common last name, but could it really be a coincidence that Rick arrived at Dune House just in time for Curtis to be killed? He knew how to dive. But how could he possibly know about the treasure? She checked the dates that he registered for a dive in the area and saw that it was a few days after Curtis' last visit. If R. Norris did stand for the same Rick Norris, then he might have visited the area not long before he traveled to Dune House with Cathy. Was that why he asked to come along with her? It made her uneasy to even consider it. If it was true, which seemed far-fetched, then Cathy could be in danger, as well as Mary and Ben. She called Mary, but her voicemail picked up.

"Mary, call me when you get this message. There's something we need to discuss."

When she hung up the phone she skimmed through the other names on the roster. None of the other names seemed familiar, but she saved a copy of the list just in case. Jim was not on the list, but it was still possible that he had visited without registering. She guessed that Curtis wouldn't risk diving without registering, because if he lost his license he wouldn't be able to teach. Then again if he'd found the treasure, he wouldn't have needed to worry about money. Confused, she decided to take a walk along the beach to try to clear her mind. The salty air refreshed her, but it did nothing to help her untangle the case. Ahead of her she caught sight of Hal and Trish. They were settled in beach chairs with a cooler between them. It could have been a cozy moment between husband and wife, but she could sense the tension between them as she approached. The wind carried their conversation towards her before she was close enough for them to notice.

"We should leave, that's what I think."

"We can't leave now, if we do you'll look guilty," Trish said.

"I'll look guilty? I didn't do anything, so why would I look guilty?"

"You keep saying you didn't do anything, but that doesn't matter. You know how these things work, you could end up in prison for something that you didn't do. If we leave, you're going to be putting a target on your back."

"Oh, bigger than the one you painted there by flirting with the idiot in the first place?" He snarled his words.

Trish shook her head. "You're crazy. It's not my fault you're crazy."

"You made me that way." He kicked some sand into the air. "Do you really think I don't know about the kiss?"

Suzie froze. She was close enough for them to notice if they turned around and saw her, but she didn't want to interrupt the conversation. She edged up along the sand away from the water, but still close enough to hear them.

"What?"

"I know. I saw you kiss him. I chose not to do anything about it, because I knew you were just waiting for any reason to leave me."

"That's not true, it's not, Hal."

"Then why did you kiss him?" He stood up from the beach chair, and in that moment he caught sight of Suzie. He flung the beach chair towards the water and shouted at Trish. "You did this, not me! You want to stay? Then you stay. I'm leaving!" He stalked off down the beach. Trish stood up and retrieved the beach chair.

"I'm sorry, Suzie. If there's any damage to it, I'll pay for it."

"You don't have to do that."

"I guess you heard all of that." She wiped at her eyes to hide the tears that Suzie could clearly see. "I've made quite a mess, haven't I?"

"It's not your fault, Trish."

"How can it not be?" She closed her eyes. "I'm so embarrassed, I guess you know everything?"

"I know that sometimes people do impulsive things."

"I wish I had never done it. I don't know why I did. I guess, I've just been lonely, and I thought maybe Curtis would be the cure for that."

"Was he?" Suzie met her eyes.

"Do you mean did I have an affair with him?"

"It's not really any of my business."

"No." She wiped at her eyes again. "He was so kind, but he turned me down. I've never felt so complimented by someone who turned me down. I was a fool, and he didn't attack me for it. He was gentle with my feelings."

"I'm glad. Curtis was a good man."

"Hal is, too. I know it doesn't seem that way, but he really is. I think part of me did flirt with Curtis to make him jealous. I just wanted him to pay more attention to me. Now, I wish I'd never done any of it. Hal could never kill anyone, I know that, but the police don't, do they?"

"I can assure you that the officer investigating the case only wants the truth, and he won't accept anything less."

"I hope that's true, because Hal didn't do this. You believe me don't you, Suzie?"

"I don't know what to believe, Trish." Suzie

studied her for a long moment. "When was the last time Hal saw Curtis?"

"I'm not really sure."

"Okay. I'll take care of the chairs. You head on back. Okay?"

"Yes, thank you, Suzie."

As she walked down the beach Suzie dialed Kirk's number. After three rings it went to voicemail.

"Kirk, this is Suzie. If you're looking at Hal as a suspect, you should know that he is planning to leave as soon as possible." She hung up the phone and slid it back into her pocket. It felt awful to rat out one of her guests, but it would feel much worse if Curtis' killer managed to escape.

Chapter Fifteen

When Suzie reached Dune House she went through the routine of checking linens, tidying the common areas, and getting some things prepared for dinner. Just as she was about to put the chicken in the oven, the front door swung open.

"Suzie?"

She turned to greet Kirk. "Hi, just give me a second." After she slid the chicken into the oven she turned back to him. "You got my message?"

"Yes, I did. Is Hal here?"

"Not right now. But I think they will be back for dinner."

"Good, maybe I'll stay, too. If that's okay?"

"Yes, of course. That might be a good idea. Listen, I need to show you something."

"All right." He sat down at the table.

"This is what I've found." Suzie slid the list

across the table to him. She had decided that Paul was right and she should tell Kirk about the shipwreck. "I know there is a shipwreck in this area, it has been confirmed by some divers, and I also know that Curtis was there the week before he came here, and the week after. I also know that a R. Norris registered to dive in the same area, just a few days before Cathy and Rick came to visit."

"Yes, but we can't be certain that it's the same person. R, could stand for anything."

"We thought maybe you could do some deeper digging to see if it was Rick. But at this point, and please don't laugh at me, we believe that Curtis might have found treasure in that shipwreck."

"What?" He tightened his lips for a moment, then cleared his throat. "Okay, I didn't laugh. Why would you come to that conclusion?"

"He was researching how to sell antiques and artifacts. He asked Cathy about how to evaluate artifacts to determine their age and worth. So obviously he had something that he wanted to evaluate."

"Or he could have been brushing up on his skills for future dives."

"Sure, he could have been. But why brush up on those skills before he found the treasure? The diver I spoke to said that anything found has to be registered in case another country has a claim to it. Maybe Curtis was trying to get around that?"

"Okay." Kirk nodded. "That is interesting. So you believe that Curtis found treasure, and then what?"

"The treasure isn't with the shipwreck anymore. Either someone took it, or Curtis moved it."

"Or it was never there in the first place. That's always a possibility isn't it?"

"Yes, of course it is. But if it was there, then it serves as good motive for people to want to kill him."

"Yes, it does. Do you think Jim knew about it?"

"There is a record of Jim diving with Curtis a few months before, but not the two most recent dives."

"Isn't it possible that Jim went diving with him and just didn't register?"

"Yes, it is possible. But he hasn't mentioned it to us," Suzie said.

"And not to me either. This is very interesting information. Unfortunately, we can't prove that there was ever actually treasure at the shipwreck, but we may not need to. I'm going to interview everyone again, and see if this new information stirs anything up."

"Ben and Cathy, too?"

"Yes Suzie. I have to be thorough."

"Okay." She nodded. "I'll let them know you need to speak with them. They're out right now, oh never mind." Suzie tilted her head towards the front door as Cathy, Ben, Rick, and Mary walked in. Ben was dripping wet from swimming. Kirk stood up as they walked further in.

"Suzie? What's going on?" Ben looked from Kirk, to his mother, then to Suzie. "Did they find Curtis' killer?"

"No Ben, not yet," Suzie said.

"I'm here to ask everyone a few more questions." Kirk looked between the three.

"Oh sure." Ben nodded. "Can I change first?"

"Yes, go ahead." Kirk looked over at Rick. "I need to speak with you again, Rick."

"Why?" Rick narrowed his eyes. "I've already spoken to you several times."

"I'm just trying to get to the bottom of what happened to Curtis. I'd like your cooperation."

"I have cooperated. I've done enough." He shoved his hands into his pockets. "I don't have anything else to say."

"I have some new questions. If you could just

step in here?" Kirk opened the door to the study.

"Rick, it's okay. I'm sure he's going to question all of us." Cathy touched Rick's arm. "Just answer his questions, it will be fine."

"Yes, I am going to question everyone. I have some new information, and I just want to go over some things to see if it sparks anything. Really, I just need your help."

"Right, until you find something that you don't like about me, and decide to put some handcuffs on me."

"I'm already not that fond of you, Rick." Kirk smiled. "And, I still haven't put handcuffs on you. Just try to relax, a few questions and you'll be on your way."

"This is ridiculous." Rick started to turn away, but Cathy patted his arm and met his eyes.

"It's all right, Rick."

"Fine." He stared at her for a moment, then followed Kirk into the study.

"Oh Mom, he's going to hate me for this."

"No, he's not." Mary rubbed her back. "If he's the kind of man that you think he is or hope he is, he will understand. Did you know about these problems he has?"

"I didn't realize they were this intense. He mentioned that there were some things that happened to him while in the service that made it difficult for him to deal with authority, but I had no idea that it was to this extent."

"Isn't it a little concerning?" Mary searched her eyes.

"It's concerning because I didn't realize it was so much of an issue. He's needed my help this whole time and I've been so caught up in us being together that I didn't even notice."

"Cathy, I know that you're fond of him, but it seems like he has a few more burdens to carry than you expected."

"Is that a polite way of telling me that you

think I shouldn't be with him? Because he's been hurt?"

"That's not what I mean at all, sweetheart. I'm just surprised, I know you're surprised, too."

"He's a good man, Mom. I know he is. Even with all that he is struggling with, deep down, he's good."

"And what if he killed Curtis?" Mary's hands clenched. "What if it turns out that he is guilty?"

"He's not, I know that he's not. He would never do something like that."

"Not even if treasure was involved?"

"What are you talking about?"

"Kirk is going to ask you about this, but Suzie and I think that Curtis might have found treasure. Real treasure. There's some evidence that Rick might have been diving in the same area where the shipwreck was found. Do you know where he was on this date?" She showed her the date on her phone.

"This is silly. I'm sure he was at college, with me." She frowned as she thought for a moment. "Actually I'm not sure that he was. He did take a few days vacation around that time. I can't be certain of the date."

"So he could have been there."

"I thought you said he was there?"

"We only have an initial and a surname."

"So you don't have proof?"

"No, I don't. But I have good reason to suspect. Not long after, he invited himself along with you here. That seems a little coincidental doesn't it?"

"It seems like a stretch, Mom. He was excited to meet you. Now I feel guilty for ever bringing him here. I never expected this from you."

"Cathy, please don't be upset with me. I am only trying to protect you."

"I'm old enough to protect myself now. I don't need you to tell me who I can or can't be with."

"I don't think that's what I was telling you. I just want you to be cautious. Please." She took her hand and met her eyes. "I'm on your side. I'm not trying to tell you what to do, I promise. Honestly, I'm sorry that this whole trip has been impacted by this. I trust your judgement, and I do like Rick, I think he probably is a good person. I just don't want to see you get hurt."

"I appreciate that, Mom, but if you really believe he could have done this, then I don't think we have anything to talk about."

The door to the study banged open and Rick stalked out of the room. "I have nothing else to say!" He headed straight for the door without even looking at Cathy.

"Rick!"

"Cathy, will you come in here with me?" Kirk stood in the doorway.

"What did you do to him?"

"I just asked him a few questions, just like I'm

going to ask you. Mary do you want to join us?"

"No, she doesn't need to." Cathy stepped into the study and closed the door behind her.

Suzie wrapped her arm around Mary and pulled her close. "Try not to worry. She's just spreading her wings."

"I get that, I do. I just don't want her to spread them with a murderer."

"Did Kirk leave?" Ben joined them near the door of the study.

"No, he's in there with Cathy."

"Oh okay."

"Do you want me to go in with you, Ben?"

"No, it's all right, Mom. I'll be fine. You should sit down, get off your knees."

"I'm fine."

"Really Mom, sit down." He gestured to the dining room table. "Relax, I'll get you some tea."

Suzie nodded and gave her friend's shoulder

a pat. "Do what your son says, he's looking out for you."

"Okay, okay." Mary sat down in her chair and sighed. As Ben walked into the kitchen, Mary leaned close. "I'm going to have to tell Kirk about Ben's shoes."

"Not unless he asks."

"Suzie."

"Mary. We know Ben didn't do this. No need to shine a spotlight on him."

"Still, it doesn't seem right."

"Here you go, Mom. I made some for you, too, Suzie."

"Thanks, Ben."

"I appreciate your time, Cathy." Kirk walked her out of the study.

"Just remember what I said, Ben." Mary frowned.

"Sure." Ben wiped his hands nervously on his

jeans. As he disappeared into the study, Cathy walked out through the front door without a word to either of them.

"She's furious with me." Mary frowned.

"She'll come around, don't worry." Suzie patted her hand. When Ben came out of the study, his face was flushed. He headed for the stairs without a word. Kirk walked up to the table and looked between the two women.

"So, you didn't know who those shoes belonged to, did you?"

"Not when you asked, I didn't." Mary gripped her cup of tea tight in her hands.

"But, after you asked Ben you discovered it didn't you?"

"Kirk, you have to understand."

"I do understand. I commend you for allowing Ben to speak up for himself. He was brave, and came forward with honesty. Of course I have to record this. It doesn't amount to enough for an arrest just yet."

"Did he tell you he has no idea how his shoes got there?"

"Yes, he did. I made a note of that, and that others had access to his shoes. We'll see what it amounts to. Take it one step at a time."

"Thanks Kirk." Suzie breathed a sigh of relief.

"No idea where Jim is?" Kirk asked.

"No sorry," Suzie said.

"I'll see if I can find him around town. I'll update you soon."

As Kirk left the house, Mary and Suzie locked eyes.

"We have to get this settled, and fast," Mary said.

"Yes, we do. If only we could find the treasure itself, maybe that would tell us something."

"Wait, you said that Curtis was looking for a cave, maybe to hide the treasure."

"Right, but the cave doesn't exist. It was a story the locals invented to keep people away from their island," Suzie replied.

"So the cave doesn't exist, but the island does?"

"Oh! Mary! That's genius!"

"Do you really think so?" Mary's eyes widened. "It was just a wild guess."

"Well, that wild guess is the only thing we have right now." Suzie glanced at her watch. "I'm going to make some calls and see if we can get a boat."

"What about Paul?"

"He's out fishing again I think, just for a few hours. I'll see if I can contact him first before I try and get a boat to take us out there."

"Okay. I'm going to go check on Ben, let me know when you find a boat."

"I will."

Suzie tried Paul but he didn't answer so she

presumed he was still out on the water. After a few phone calls to try and get a boat, she came up with nothing. Most of the people who had a boat were tied up in jobs, or unavailable for other reasons. She recalled a friend of Paul's she'd met a few months back. He was a nice enough guy, and Paul seemed to trust him. They had grown up in Garber together. However, she didn't know his number. He might be out at sea but it was worth a shot to try him. She sent a text to Mary.

Let's head down to the docks.

Mary appeared a few minutes later, her forehead creased in concern.

"How's Ben?" Suzie led her out of Dune House and into the parking lot.

"Not good. Apparently Kirk put quite a scare into him. He said that he's having Ben's shoes DNA tested for DNA that doesn't match Ben's. He also said that Ben's fingerprints were found in the dive shack, and on Curtis' equipment."

"But that shouldn't be surprising, Ben was

one of his students," Suzie said.

"I know it shouldn't be, but this is a path that Kirk is following. We need to find out the truth as quickly as possible."

"We're going to."

Chapter Sixteen

Suzie drove down to the docks and parked in the far lot. After checking that Paul's boat wasn't docked she walked along the dock with Mary until she found Shawn's boat. He was on the deck scrubbing down some equipment when she spotted him.

"Shawn!" Suzie smiled and waved to him. He looked a little confused at first, and she realized that he didn't recognize her. "Suzie, Paul's girlfriend, remember?"

"Oh right, hi Suzie." He smiled.

"This is my friend, Mary. We were wondering if you might be able to do us a favor?"

"What?" His eyes narrowed slightly.

"We want to find the secret island, Bucky's Island."

"Oh, why would you want to find that place?" He laughed. "That's for teenagers."

"We have our reasons. Will you take us out please?"

"Why didn't you ask Paul?"

"He's out fishing at the moment."

"All right, I'll take you out. But I don't want Paul having a problem with me. So if any of this goes sideways, you're going to tell him why, not me."

"Don't worry. Paul won't care."

"Okay, let's head out." He helped them both onto the boat.

"Is it far off shore?"

"Not at all. Bucky's Island has been a local secret for a long time."

"I can't believe I never heard of it until a few days ago." Suzie raised an eyebrow.

"No, you wouldn't have, you didn't grow up here. Only locals have ever heard of it, and not even all of the locals. Mostly just kids that grew up with houses on the beach itself. It's basically a tiny little island, well we call it an island, but it's not even big enough to be considered an island. Anyway, it's where the teens would go to hang out when I was younger. These days it's mostly empty because of all of the new rules about teens and watercraft. Once in a while some locals will go out there for a picnic or to hang out, but there are so many nicer places to go, that it isn't used much. It won't take us long to get there."

Suzie watched as the docks grew distant. She could only hope that the secret island would be the lead that they needed. About twenty minutes later Mary pointed across the water.

"Is that it?" She shielded her eyes.

"It must be." Suzie saw the tiny bit of land with a small amount of foliage to separate it from the sea.

"Looks empty as usual." Shawn pulled up as close as he could to the shore. "It's too shallow for me to get any closer. Do you want to come back with a raft?"

"No, we can wade our way in. Right Mary?"

"Uh, sure." Mary nodded.

"I'll go first." Suzie climbed down the ladder on the side of the boat and into the water, then she turned back to help Mary. "Here Mary." Suzie offered her a hand as she tried to climb down from the ship.

"No, it's okay I can do it." Mary waved her off. In the process she slid down the last rung of the ladder and landed with a splash in the shallow water. "Ugh. Suzie, stop laughing and help me up!"

"I'm sorry, it was just so cute when you gasped. Are you okay?" She helped her to her feet. Once steady, Mary rolled her eyes.

"Yes, I'm okay. Just bruised pride as usual."

"Well, we're both soaked now, we might as well go get sandy." Suzie led her through the water to the shore.

"I wish I was as agile as you."

"A few more doctor's visits might help."

"Now you sound like Ben."

"Your son has a point, Mary. You can't ignore that pain forever."

"I can for a little while longer." She grinned. "I'm holding out for the cute surgeon."

"I bet you are." Suzie laughed. "All right, we're here. Now what?"

"Well, without a diver we can't search the water, but I guess we can take a look around the island. Maybe Curtis left something behind that will give us a clue."

"That would be nice. It's not like we have much territory to cover." As Suzie stood at the edge of the water, she could clearly see the shore on the other side of the island. There were a few trees and bushes, but not enough to hide much. As they picked their way through the island, she became discouraged.

"Honestly, Mary, I think this was a mistake.

There's nothing here to find. Maybe Curtis just came out here to blow off steam. One of the locals probably told him about it."

"That's possible, but I don't think we should give up just yet. We didn't look over there." She pointed to a section of the island which was furthest from where the boat was anchored. Suzie nodded and followed Mary's lead. As they approached Suzie noticed strange dips and rises in the sand. She paused beside a pile of large gray rocks. They seemed out of place on the island to begin with, but the way they were stacked seemed even more odd.

"What do you think this is about?" Suzie stared at the rocks.

"Let's see." Mary moved one of the rocks, then another. Suzie joined her, and soon they were almost through the pile. When Suzie moved the last of the rocks, Mary stared down into a deep hole beneath it.

"Oh my! Suzie!" Mary looked up from the

hole. "Is that what I think it is?"

"Yes, it is." Suzie looked over her shoulder to ensure that there was no one else on the island with them. When she looked back down into the hole she was startled again by the pile of coins at the bottom. There were scattered gems and necklaces as well, but the coins took up the majority of the space. "Curtis must have moved the treasure here to keep it safe. He probably thought no one would ever look for it here."

"We seriously just found buried treasure?" Mary shook her head.

"Sh! Not so loud. We don't want Shawn to hear us."

"Why, do you think he would try to take it?"

"It's very possible that those coins are worth a large amount of money. When it comes to riches, you can never predict who is going to do what to get to them. So yes, I do think it's very possible."

"What are we going to do? Should we take

them? Should we call Kirk?"

"No." Suzie peered out over the water, then began to move the rocks back into place to hide the treasure. "Not until we find out who killed Curtis."

"Why?" Mary frowned.

"Because the moment we tell Kirk about this treasure, everyone will care about it. He'll have to process it as evidence, and there is a chance that everyone in town will hear about it. Any chance we have of getting a confession out of the killer will be gone. If we keep this to ourselves, just you and me, then we can decide when we want to reveal it. If we do it the right way, we might be able to flush out the killer."

"Okay, I think I understand. Here, let me help." Mary shoved a few of the rocks back into place as well.

"Remember, not a word to Shawn."

"I'll remember."

When they waded back out to the boat, Shawn helped them up onto it.

"How did it go, lady pirates?" He grinned.

"You were right, there was nothing out there. I think we made a mistake."

"Oh well, at least you got a nice boat ride, right?"

"Right." Suzie nodded. She and Mary sat on the bench seat closest to the back of the boat. It was still hard for Suzie to believe that they found the treasure. A part of her wondered if it might have actually been some kind of prank that one of the local kids played. Maybe those coins weren't as real as they looked. When they reached the dock and Suzie stepped off the boat, she caught sight of Paul. He held out his hand to her. She took it with a smile.

"I can't believe you would cheat on me." He did not return the smile.

"What?" She stared at him.

"Seriously Suzie, did you really think you were going to get away with this?"

"Hey Paul, it wasn't like that at all, I swear." Shawn stepped off the boat after Mary.

"It sure looks like what I think it is." Paul looked from Shawn to Suzie. "You went out on another man's boat? What's wrong with my boat?" He grinned.

Suzie relaxed and laughed. "Sorry Paul, I didn't know when you'd be back."

"No need to apologize." He nodded to Shawn. "Thanks for taking her out."

"Oh sure, anytime." Shawn breathed a sigh of relief.

"I think I scared him." Paul laughed as he walked with Mary and Suzie along the dock. Suzie longed to tell him about what they found, but she thought he would think she was crazy, and if she wasn't crazy then she didn't want to put him in danger.

"So, can you join us for dinner tonight?" Suzie looked into Paul's eyes.

"I would love that." Paul nodded. "But I have to go out again on the boat tonight, so I might have to leave dinner early, is that okay?"

"Absolutely!" Suzie smiled.

"Great." He kissed her cheek, waved to Mary, and walked back off to his boat. The moment Suzie and Mary were alone in the car they could only talk about the treasure and what it could mean. The entire way back to Dune House they debated how the treasure could help them find the killer. Once in the kitchen with two cups of coffee they continued to discuss it.

"Well, our best guess at this point is that whoever killed Curtis was after the treasure. So why don't we let the killer show himself, or herself?" Mary fiddled with her cup of coffee.

"How?" Suzie leaned forward.

"All of the suspects probably now know that

there was a shipwreck and possibly treasure. They've all been questioned about their knowledge of it, and so they can assume that Curtis was in possession of it if it existed."

"Okay." Suzie nodded. "I'm listening."

"What they don't know, is that we know where it is. No one knows. Right? Not even Paul?'

"Right. Not even the kids?"

"Right. So, why don't we let it slip that we know where the treasure is? Whoever killed Curtis is likely to come after us."

"Wait, even if we ignore for the moment just how dangerous that would be, we can't know that the killer will come after us. It's possible that Curtis was killed out of jealousy, by either Hal or Trish," Suzie said.

"It is possible, and if no one comes after the treasure then we may want to lean more towards Hal and Trish. No matter what we're going to get some kind of response. Either someone will come after us to try to find the treasure, or no one will, in which case we can zero in more on Hal and Trish."

"What about Rick and Jim? Do you really think they'd come after us?"

"If one of them is a murderer, then yes." Mary frowned. "I know it's a risky idea. Usually I wouldn't even consider it. But Kirk is focusing in on Ben, and I want this settled once and for all."

"Then we will have to be very careful."

Chapter Seventeen

After dinner Suzie washed the dishes. She had the kitchen window open. As Ben approached the back door, she could hear his conversation with someone on the phone.

"I told you, I'll take care of it. You can trust me. I have more than enough. Just tell him that this needs to be it. I want him to leave me alone after this."

Suzie closed her eyes as she listened to Ben's words. She didn't want to suspect him, but it was hard not to. How could Ben, who was strapped for cash suddenly have enough to pay off the debt to his loan shark? Was it possible that Curtis told him about the treasure? It made her feel sick to even consider it. When he stepped through the back door she focused on the dishes.

"Hey Ben." She smiled at him.

"Hey Aunt Suzie. Want some help with

those?"

"No, it's okay. How are you doing?"

"All right." He shrugged. "Just starting to wonder when all of this is going to be settled."

"Yes, I think we all are. Listen, we're having a bonfire tonight. I'd like for you to be there for it."

"Sure. I love a bonfire. Want help with the fire?"

"I'll let you know."

"Great. I'll let Cathy and Rick know."

Suzie stared after him as he walked away. She was tempted to question him about his phone conversation, but she decided against it. They would know the truth soon enough. As she finished the dishes she realized the only person who wasn't at dinner was Jim. Paul and Kirk had spent some time on the porch, then Kirk left early. She had no idea what they discussed, but Paul appeared less than pleased as he kissed her goodnight and headed home. She purposely didn't tell him about the bonfire. She wanted him as far from danger as possible.

Now she needed to find Jim, but she had no idea where he was. It was still light outside. He could be diving for all she knew, but she did see him walk out onto the beach earlier and hadn't noticed him return. Her heart fluttered as she thought about being out on the isolated beach so far away from Dune House. The beaches in town were more popular for tourists and residents alike. The more isolated beaches tended to be rocky and not as friendly to visitors.

The further she walked, the more she wondered if she was mistaken about Jim coming out this way. Even if he was diving there should be some sign of him being there. She was just about to turn back, when she heard a splash from behind a pile of rocks. The rocks were stacked high enough to shield from view whatever was happening beyond them. She held her breath as she crept forward. She wanted to see Jim, before he saw her. As she rounded the rocks she got a full view of him, as he slung water from his hair and rose up out of the water. Her eyes widened as she took in the sight of every inch of his skin. Jim was a very fit man, and though she hadn't noticed before, she now realized that he was quite muscular as well. She was so stunned by discovering him in the nude that she couldn't look away as he began to turn back towards the shore.

"Oh!" He laughed. "Suzie, you startled me." He covered himself and backed up towards the rocks. "I didn't expect anyone to be out here."

"I'm sorry." She blinked as she realized she was staring, and backed away from the edge of the water. Only then did she notice his clothes neatly folded on one of the rocks.

"Would you mind?" He gestured to a towel on the rock beside his clothes. Her heart raced as she did her best not to look at him. She grabbed the towel and held it out to him as she looked away. "I'm sorry about this, really. I expected to be alone." He wrapped the towel around his waist and walked out of the water. She was so flustered she could barely bring herself to speak, but finally managed to put some words together.

"This is not a nude beach, Jim."

"I realize that. Are you going to call the cops on me?" He laughed. The laughter faded when she didn't respond. "Suzie, I'm sorry. I'm used to being on beaches where nudity is allowed. Honestly, whenever I'm feeling down, I go for a swim in the nude. It's so refreshing. Have you ever tried it?"

"That's not the point."

"Hm. You should try it some time. It feels like every trouble you have is being washed away. Cleansed."

She glanced over at him for a moment. Was the swim his way of cleansing himself after murdering his friend? "I'm sure it is, but I'm familiar with what a jellyfish sting feels like."

"Oh absolutely." He laughed. "I've experienced that, too. But, it's still worth it. Anyway, I'm sorry again. I didn't mean to disturb you this way."

"It's all right."

"What are you doing all the way out here anyway? I hunted this place down thinking it would be private enough."

"I was actually looking for you."

"Well, you certainly found me." He raised an eyebrow.

"Yes, I did." Suzie laughed and dared to meet his eyes. His sparkled, as if he was more amused by her discomfort than by getting caught. "We're having a bonfire tonight, for all of our guests. It's just a way we'd like to relieve some of the tension in the house, and also to honor Curtis. He loved to have bonfires on the beach."

"Yes, he was always a firebug." He nodded, and the amusement in his eyes faded. "I do miss

238

that man."

"I'm sure you do, Jim. I hope you'll join us tonight, at sunset."

"Yes, I think I will."

"Great. I'll see you then." She cleared her throat.

"Less of me." Jim winked. "I promise."

"Yes, that would probably be best." Suzie felt her cheeks heat up as she turned away. It was hard to get the image of Jim rising out of the water out of her mind. However, the more she thought about his behavior the more strange she thought it was. Was it really normal to swim in the nude when you were grieving for a friend? She'd done some wild things in her life, but those two activities didn't seem to blend together to her. She reminded herself not to judge.

***

Mary walked into the dining room and spotted Hal and Trish out on the deck on the side of the house. Since the door had been repaired the space was being utilized more. She opened the door to the deck just as Hal wrapped his arms around his wife.

"You know I'll always love you." He stared into her eyes. "No matter what you put me through."

"You're going to have to forgive me properly one day, Hal."

"Probably." He looked up as Mary stepped through the door. "Mary." He nodded as he stepped away from Trish.

"I'm sorry to interrupt. I wanted to let you know that we're going to have a bonfire tonight and I would like for you to be there. This is still your vacation, even though it's been hindered by tragedy. I feel like we've all been waiting for the murder to be solved, but we think this is a nice way to honor Curtis, and I think we are still entitled to enjoy some of the beauty that this place has to offer. Will you be there?"

"I don't know." Trish looked out over the water. "It might be awkward."

"It won't be. It's about joining together. I know the investigation is still ongoing, but just for one night I want to see if we can let go of that, and bask in the moonlight. At least come and see how it feels. If it isn't comfortable you can always leave."

"Won't that make me look even more guilty?" Hal rolled his eyes. "It seems to me that if I sneeze I'm one step away from handcuffs."

"That's the point of the bonfire. To help everyone relax a little, and to remind us that we're all here to enjoy each other's company and honor Curtis."

"I'll think about it." Hal took Trish's hand. "It might be nice to spend some time beside a fire on the beach, don't you think?"

"I think it's ridiculous." Trish turned back to face Mary. "We're talking about the same beach where Curtis died. Don't you think that's a little morbid?"

"I don't think so. Curtis loved the water. I think it would be a nice way to honor him."

"Even if the killer is among those honoring him?" Trish narrowed her eyes. "Someone here did it."

"We don't know that. All we know is that Curtis lost his life long before he should have."

"I guess you're right about that." Trish shrugged. "We'll be there."

"All right, good." Mary smiled at them both, then walked around to the front porch. As she reached it, Suzie climbed up the front steps.

"Well?"

"I've spoken to Trish, and Hal. I think they are going to be there."

"I spoke to Ben and he is going to talk to Cathy and Rick."

"Great," Mary said. "Did you find Jim?"

"Yes I did." Suzie hoped her cheeks weren't flushed as she recalled the way she found him. "He said he would be there."

"What is it? Did something happen?" Mary studied her.

"Let's just say, Jim has a very strange way of grieving. I also invited Louis. I thought he might enjoy it and the group might relax more to have someone there that wasn't staying at Dune House and isn't a suspect in the crime, as far as we know at least."

"Are you sure we shouldn't invite Kirk?"

"No way, we can't invite him. If we do, everyone is going to clam up. No, I think we have everyone right where we want them to be. Now we just need marshmallows, graham crackers, and chocolate."

"What?" Mary blinked.

"You can't have a bonfire without s'mores, now can you?"

"Good point. I'll round up some sticks we can use to toast them."

As the two walked into Dune House, Suzie glanced back over her shoulder. She could see Jim approaching along the beach. He walked with ease as the light breeze from the water fluttered his unbuttoned shirt.

Chapter Eighteen

Just as the sun began to set, Suzie and Mary huddled in the kitchen.

"Are you sure about this, Suzie?"

"Yes. I think it's the best idea we could come up with, and we can't waste any more time on trying to come up with something. Kirk is not going to be able to make or convince everyone to stay much longer, and once everyone begins to scatter, it's possible that the case is going to go cold."

"That would be terrible."

"Yes, it would. So we try this tonight, and see if it's going to lead us to discovering something. If it doesn't, we haven't lost anything."

"Okay, well the s'more supplies are ready." Mary glanced at the sky. "It's just about sunset. Are we ready?"

"Yes. You have the coordinates on your phone

already, right?"

"Yes. I left them on the screen so whoever picks up the phone will be able to find them right away."

"Good. Remember to leave it in plain sight, but try to block it as you walk away so that no one will notice it right away and remind you to pick it up."

"That shouldn't be a problem. My hips are big enough they can hide anything."

"Mary!" Suzie shook her head.

"Sorry." She laughed. "I'm nervous. I get silly when I'm nervous."

"It's okay. I'm nervous, too. Let's try to go into this with as open minds as possible. I know that we have our own suspicions, but hopefully tonight will give us a solid lead."

"Is the shack all set up?"

"Yes it is, and so is the camera."

"Perfect." Mary smiled. "Who knew we could

be so tech savvy?"

"Louis might have helped."

"But we knew to ask him for help, that's something, right?" Mary laughed.

"Hmm, I think I could get used to you being nervous. You're quite funny."

"Ugh, if you could feel how fast my heart is racing you wouldn't wish it on me, trust me."

"Just try to relax. We know what we're doing, and we're going to be perfectly safe."

"I'm trying." Mary nodded.

"I'm going to go get the fire started."

"Okay I'll be down in a little bit with drinks and supplies."

"Great." Suzie stepped out of the house and walked down towards the beach. It didn't take long for her to get the bonfire set up. However, as the flames began to crackle, her own heart started to race. She wasn't nervous about the plan working, she was nervous about the plan failing.

If no one took the bait, they would still have no solid suspect, and Curtis' death might hang over all of them for the rest of their lives.

***

The flames crackled in the silence that filled the air. No one was interested in talking. The glow of the fire painted each face with sinister shadows. It was difficult not to think about who the killer might be. Suzie stirred the embers, then looked up at the group.

"So, I guess everyone knows that we think that Curtis was treasure hunting."

"Not surprising." Jim grinned. "He always believed he would find something."

"Do you think he ever did?" Mary looked up from the fire.

"I don't think so, I think if he did he would have told me about it. What do you think?" Jim asked.

"What would I know about it?" Mary

shrugged and laughed nervously.

"Sh, Mary!" Suzie frowned.

"Uh oh, you two are up to something." Ben grinned. "I can always tell when you're hiding something."

"That's what he thinks." Cathy shook her head. "Mom and Suzie are just trying to lighten the mood and get our minds off the tragedy."

"Is it working?" Suzie glanced over at Hal and Trish who were huddled together. "I know that this has been difficult for all of us. But maybe the romantic idea of treasure being hidden somewhere nearby will lighten the mood."

"Maybe." Trish sighed. "But I could care less about treasure. I'm more interested in time travel. I'd love to correct my mistakes."

"I think we all would." Ben nodded and added some kindling to the fire.

"I heard a rumor that Curtis might have hidden treasure somewhere nearby." Mary fiddled with her phone. "Suzie and I are looking into it."

"That's silly." Jim laughed. "If Curtis found treasure, he wouldn't have hidden it, he would have flaunted it. Where do these rumors say the treasure might be?"

"Not a word, Mary, that's between us." Suzie pointed a finger in her direction.

"Suzie, it's not a big deal. It's not like we're actually going to be able to find it."

"We might. You don't know. We have the coordinates..."

"Suzie, now who's saying too much?"

"You're right, let's have s'mores." Suzie began to prepare the snacks.

"Wait a minute, are you saying you have an idea of where the treasure is." Rick sat forward. "Do you know that some divers spend decades looking for treasure? If you have reason to believe the treasure might be hidden around here somewhere, I could dive for it."

"Why you?" Jim stared at him. "If Curtis found treasure, I'm the one who should be looking for it."

"Anyone can hire a diver." Hal smirked. "The two of you don't get to claim it just because you're trained."

"Never mind any of that." Mary huffed. "We're here to join together, not argue. I'm sure there isn't really treasure. If there was, we would all know about it. Like Jim said, Curtis would have told him."

"Right." Jim stared into the fire. "He would have."

As the bonfire wound down, Mary stood up from her beach chair. "My knees are getting sore. I think I'm going to head in."

"I'll clean up." Suzie offered.

"Mom, I'll walk you up to the house." Ben stood up to join her.

"It's all right, I'm fine," Mary said.

"No, I'll go with you." Cathy looped an arm around her mother's waist. The two made their way towards the house.

Trish gathered some of the left-over s'more supplies. "I'll take these up to the kitchen."

"Thanks Trish." Suzie noticed Mary's cell phone left behind on her chair, but she didn't look directly at it. "I'll put out this fire. Would one of you bring up the chairs?"

"We can work together." Hal stretched his arms.

As Suzie put out the fire, the beach was plunged into darkness. It was a cloudy night without a lot of illumination. In the shadows she couldn't tell who folded up Mary's chair, but not one of them mentioned finding her phone. As they headed up the beach with the chairs, she checked the sand to be sure it hadn't been left behind. Without any sign of it, she could only guess that someone had taken the bait.

After putting away the chairs Suzie headed up the beach a short distance to the dive shack. Once inside she could see the camera pointed at the beach. It wouldn't take long before whoever took the phone figured out that the coordinates led directly to the shack. A few minutes later, Mary joined her in the shack. They were quiet as they waited to see who took the bait. Almost an hour slipped by.

"Maybe no one did." Mary frowned. "Does that mean it was Hal or Trish?"

"Maybe no one noticed your phone and it's still folded up in one of the chairs."

"Ugh, if so we're back to square one."

Just then, a figure came into view on the video feed. Suzie grabbed Mary's arm. Somehow the person had slipped past them and was right outside the dive shack. Mary flicked off the video monitor to prevent any light from shining. The door knob to the shack began to twist. Suzie held her breath as the figure stepped inside. All they needed was to see his face. Once they saw it, they could go to Kirk with a genuine suspect. But the shack was dim, and although the figure was definitely male it was hard to detect any other characteristics. He began to shove furniture and equipment aside. He stomped on the floorboards. There was no question that he was looking for something. Mary and Suzie huddled further back in their hiding place.

"Suzie, what if he finds us?" Mary hissed.

"Sh!" Suzie tightened her grip on Mary's arm. She had planned that they would slip out the back before the murderer got inside, but he'd gotten inside so fast that there was no time to escape. He shoved aside the pile of boxes that they hid behind, and stared down into their frightened faces.

"Was this some kind of trap?" Jim glared at them. "Where's the treasure?"

"It was just a joke." Mary cleared her throat. "Something to lighten the mood."

"Some joke." He snarled and grabbed Suzie by the arm. When he pulled her to her feet, she had to swallow back a scream. The gun he had tucked into his waistband silenced her. "I know that Curtis found treasure. He stole it from me. It belonged to both of us. But he lied and said there wasn't any treasure there. Then he went back and got it, to keep it for himself. That treasure is rightfully mine."

"So you murdered him?" Suzie stared at him. "Why would you kill him? He was the only one who could tell you where the treasure was."

"Because he told me that it was in a secret underwater cave. Once I knew where it was, I killed him. He deserved it. He stole from me, he betrayed me, and he thought he could get away with it. But imagine my surprise when I found out that he really was nothing but a liar, and there was no cave!"

"Jim, calm down." Suzie studied him. "We can help you out of this."

"Oh, you're going to help me all right. Now, you're going to tell me exactly where the treasure is." His voice sent shivers down Mary's spine. She held her breath for a moment to keep from gasping. "Need some motivation?" He shoved Suzie hard into the wall. Suzie slumped to the floor, unconscious. "She's going to be your motivation. If you," he pointed at Mary, "don't take me to the treasure, she's not going to survive." He grabbed some rope and tied Suzie up, then opened one of the cylinders on the floor beside her. "Those fumes are going to kill her in an hour. That's how long you've got." He turned back to Mary. "So what's it going to be? Are you going to tell me where the treasure is and save both of you, or are you going to die right here with her?"

"I'll show you. But we need a boat."

"Luckily, I have a boat. I was going out diving again." Jim pulled her out of the shack. Her eyes blurred with tears at the thought of Suzie alone in the shack. When she felt the heel of his hand push against the back of her shoulder she forced herself to take a step forward. "Where is it? Tell me, or you're never going to see Suzie again."

"You can't do this. Jim, I know you're a good man, deep down."

"Am I?" He laughed. "The only thing I know I am about to be, is a rich man. Now, tell me where the treasure is. Time is running out for your friend."

"Okay, but I can't tell you. I have to take you there."

"Why?" He narrowed his eyes.

"It's not on any map, and it's hidden."

"Well, isn't that convenient. Fine, let's go then." He grabbed her by the elbow and pulled her down the beach. Mary's heart raced when she spotted a couple on a stroll along the beach. She opened her mouth to scream, but he squeezed her arm hard before she could. "One noise, one word, and Suzie is going to lose her best friend."

"I won't say anything." Mary recalled the gun in his waistband and closed her eyes. She clenched her teeth despite the terror that rushed through her.

"Good. We're going to the dock. Take your car."

Mary did as he instructed and opened the door to the car that she shared with Suzie. Her hands trembled as she gripped the steering wheel. All she could think of was Suzie back in the shack, all alone. She didn't have her phone, since that was part of the ploy, so she had no way to alert anyone to Suzie's plight.

"How long does she have?"

"Never mind that. Just drive."

Mary drove fast, but Jim patted her knee. "Slow down. I don't want us getting pulled over. No tricks."

"Sorry." She bit into her bottom lip and

parked at the dock. He led her down to the end of the dock to a small boat, and instructed her to get on. She did as she was told and gave him the general direction to go. She didn't want to tell him too much, as she knew her usefulness, and in turn Suzie's, would disappear the moment he found the treasure. After some time motoring across the open water, Jim stared hard at her.

"Where are we going, Mary?"

"There." She pointed to the island and shivered. She could have lied and led him somewhere else, but she didn't want to risk Suzie's life. She only hoped that the time they spent getting to the island would be enough for something miraculous to happen. As he edged the boat close to the island she wondered if this would be the last place she would ever see. It was pretty, at least. She drank in the sight of the moon and the stars as they illuminated the water below. The sky had begun to clear.

"Let's go." He turned the boat off and dropped

an inflatable boat down into the water. "You first." Mary struggled to get over the side of the boat, and landed awkwardly. Jim jumped in after her, and paddled them towards the shore. Mary considered trying to wrench a paddle from him, but she knew she wasn't strong enough to overcome him. When they reached the shore, Jim climbed out first. "Where?"

"I'll show you."

"No. Just tell me."

"I can't, it's too hard to describe. I have to show you."

"Fine. Let's go."

"Wait." She climbed out of the boat. "What's to stop you from leaving me here and never going back to save Suzie?"

"This." He held up her phone. "Once I have the treasure, I will give you this. You can call for help, I don't care, I'll be long gone. None of this would have been necessary if Rick had taken the fall like he was supposed to."

"What do you mean?"

"I planted his shoes in that shack so that the local police would think he was the killer. But they're not even smart enough to do that."

Her stomach churned. He'd taken Ben's shoes by mistake because they were in his room and the same size as Rick's. But what if he hadn't? She came to the awful realization that she would have believed Rick was a killer if it was his shoes that Kirk found in the shack.

"He was your friend, Jim. Why did you do this to him?"

"Friends don't lie and cheat. The only good thing that ever happened in my life was finding that shipwreck. I thought Curtis was protecting me when he said I shouldn't go down, that it was too dangerous. But the truth was, he wanted to take the treasure for himself. He lied about there being nothing there, and then stole it right out from under me. I deserved it just as much as he did. But instead of being my friend, he was a thief. He deserved what he got."

"But I don't understand. You never left your room. Did you have a partner?"

"There's more than one way to leave a room you know. I am experienced at abseiling, remember? I used the ropes that Curtis had of mine to abseil down the outside of the building, I tampered with Curtis' equipment, then I climbed back up. Really, Curtis killed himself. He should have checked his equipment before he went diving, but he was always making stupid mistakes like that. If he had checked it, he would still be alive. But he didn't, and now he's dead. Your friend is going to be the next to die if you don't show me where that treasure is."

"Over there." She whispered as she pointed across the island. "Under the rocks."

Together they walked towards them. Mary wanted to believe that he would give her the phone, but she doubted it. When they reached the rocks, his tone became nastier.

"Is this some kind of trick?" Jim stared at her. "You move them."

"I don't know if I can move them all."

"You'd better make your best effort." He gestured to the rocks.

"All right, all right, I'll try." She grabbed the rock on the top and heaved it aside. Maybe Paul would wonder where Suzie was, maybe Ben or Cathy would decide to go looking for her. Someone had to do something, because she had a very strong feeling that Jim was not going to let her go.

"Let's go, move it." Jim gave her a light shove from behind.

Mary pushed the last of the rocks aside, then stood back. Her heart lurched as she realized that the moment he saw the treasure, she would become nothing but a liability to him. As he walked up to the edge of the hole she glanced around in search of anything that she might be able to use as a weapon. She could try to run, even with her bad knees, but the island was so small, and there was nowhere to hide.

Chapter Nineteen

"I knew it." Jim stared down into the hole. "I knew it!" He turned towards Mary with wide eyes and red cheeks. "You're a liar!"

"What?" Mary took a step back and stumbled on one of the rocks as Jim advanced on her.

"Where is the treasure? I thought you cared about your friend, but I was wrong. Now if you don't tell me where the treasure is I'm going to go back to that old house and reunite your son and daughter with their dear aunt. Do you understand me?"

"No wait, please. The treasure should be there. That's where it was when we found it." Mary made her way to the edge of the hole and looked inside. Nothing but a pit of sand greeted her. She crouched down and dug in the sand. The further she dug, the more her hands shook. If the treasure was gone, then she had no way of protecting Suzie, or her children. Nothing would stop Jim from going after them all. "Someone must have taken it." She closed her eyes.

"Someone? Who could? I thought you said only Suzie and you knew where the treasure was? Or was that a lie, too?"

"No, it was the truth. I thought we were the only ones, but someone must have found out about it."

"Or maybe Suzie isn't the trustworthy friend that you thought she was." He laughed. "Just like Curtis. He wanted to keep all of the money for himself. Suzie probably moved the treasure so that she would have it for herself. How does that feel?"

"She wouldn't." Mary shook her head.

"That's what I thought, too. But look how that turned out. Honestly, I feel sorry for you. I know what it feels like to be betrayed by someone you considered to be a friend. But none of that matters right now. All that matters is me getting that treasure. No matter how much sympathy I have for you, please understand, I will not hesitate to do whatever it takes to get it."

"Just let me talk to her. If you let me talk to her, I'm sure she'll tell me where the treasure is. If she knows that you're threatening me, or Ben, or Cathy, she'll do anything to keep us safe. Please, just let me talk to her."

"Fine. I will. But that's the last chance either of you are going to have." He grabbed her arm and pulled her back towards the boat.

Mary was certain that Suzie hadn't moved the treasure, but at the very least she would be able to see her friend again. As they headed back towards the boat, Mary heard something splash in the water not far from her. She glanced to the side, and spotted a small rock as it landed in the water. She looked up and saw a police boat, hidden by the shadows of one of the few trees. Instantly she knew what to do. She lunged away from Jim, and suddenly the entire island lit up with the flashing lights of the police boat. Jim was tackled to the ground by an officer while Kirk shouted at him to stay down.

"He has a gun!" Mary gasped. She watched as the officer wrestled the gun out of Jim's hands. She had no idea how Kirk found her, but tears of relief spilled down her cheeks. "Suzie! Someone has to help Suzie." She breathlessly explained Suzie's location. Kirk barked into his radio, then wrapped an arm around Mary.

"It's okay, Mary. We're going to take care of her. Let's get you off this island."

After a few minutes on the boat Kirk walked over to her.

"Suzie has been found. She's fine. There were no dangerous fumes, I think that Jim was trying to scare you. She was just knocked out."

"Oh, thank goodness." She pressed her hand against her chest. "But how did you find us? And where is the treasure?"

"I got notification during dinner that they

managed to trace the last call that Curtis made the morning of his death and it was to a pawn broker so that heightened my suspicions that he might have had treasure. I also found out that R. Norris was not Rick it was a different diver so I didn't think that Rick was the murderer, but I wasn't sure. After Suzie mentioned the cave, and that Curtis might be looking for a hiding place, I thought about this island. When I spoke with Paul after dinner, he mentioned you and Suzie going out on a boat with Shawn. I thought it was strange. So I decided to take a look at the island myself. I found and confiscated the treasure. I knew that the killer would come looking for the treasure eventually, so I kept a patrol on it. When they spotted you and Jim they alerted me. It's a good thing they did, because you could have been killed, Mary."

"I know." She sighed and wiped at her eyes. "It was a risk I had to take."

"I wish you had come to me first. Now that we

have Curtis' killer, it's hard to be upset. I understand you were worried about Ben, but your life matters, too."

"Thanks Kirk." She smiled at him as the boat pulled up to the docks. Jim was led off in handcuffs. The moment Mary stepped off the boat Suzie ran towards her. She threw her arms around her friend.

"Oh, Mary I'm so sorry. I never should have let you be in such danger."

"We had our reasons, Suzie." She filled her in on what Jim told her about Curtis taking the treasure for himself, and how he was able to escape from his room without being seen.

"It's hard to believe we were under the same roof as a murderer all this time."

"But all that matters is that we're all safe now." She saw her son as he approached from the parking lot. "Almost all of us. Kirk, do you have a minute to talk with me and Ben? He has a difficult matter he's dealing with."

"Sure." He nodded. "Anything that I can do to help, I'm here."

"Thanks." She hugged Ben. "I want you to come with me and speak to Kirk so we can sort out your little problem."

"I don't know, Mom. Dad gave me more money so I have some more time."

"No, we need to solve this once and for all so you can put it behind you. Trust me."

"Okay." Ben nodded. Mary put her arm around him and led him off to speak with Kirk.

Suzie rubbed her head where she'd collided with the wall. Paul walked up to her in the midst of all of the flashing lights.

"What's going on here?"

Suzie filled him in on the events, the arrest, and being left in the shack. "I came to when Ben found me. Kirk called him because he knew he would be the closest. Poor Mary must have been beside herself."

"I'm so glad that you're safe." He looked into her eyes. "Shortly after I docked I heard all of the sirens, it scared me. I knew something was up."

"I'm sorry, in all of the chaos I should have called you, but I wanted to make sure Mary was safe, it was all I was thinking about."

"I understand."

"What do you think they'll do with the treasure?"

"I don't know. Once they decide who it belongs to, they'll go from there."

"I'm just so glad this is over." Suzie hugged him. "Now, finally Curtis can have some peace."

"He was lucky to have you as a friend, Suzie." He kissed the top of her head.

"Ouch!"

"Oops, sorry." He smiled and kissed her cheek instead. "Next time, keep me in the loop, hmm?"

"Yes, I will, Paul. I just wanted to keep you safe, so I thought the less you knew the better."

"I'd like to be able to do the same for you once in a while. I'm not sure how you think you can keep me safe, when you're always putting my heart at such risk."

"What do you mean?"

"I mean, you carry my heart with you, Suzie, whether you know that or not. When you're in danger, it's in danger."

"That's sweet." Suzie smiled at him. He had such a rugged exterior with his broad shoulders, curly hair, big bushy eyebrows and weathered skin that he always surprised her with his sensitivity.

"It's the truth. So the next time you think you're protecting me, please try to remember, whenever you take a risk with yourself, you're taking a risk with my heart, too."

"I'll remember." She gazed into his eyes. "And I promise not to cheat on you anymore."

"Good, because Shawn was going to pay for

that."

"Stop!" She laughed. He hugged her again. Over his shoulder she saw Hal and Trish huddled close in the parking lot. All of the commotion had woken up just about the entire town of Garber. The two clung to each other. Suzie realized that their relationship might not be perfect, but it was still strong. Hal had a checkered past, and a bit of a temper. Trish had a wandering eye, and a desire for a little drama. But they loved each other, and in the end, stuck together through a very difficult time. Just as Mary and Ben walked away from Kirk, Cathy and Rick walked up to them. Mary offered her hand to Rick.

"I'm sorry for doubting you, Rick."

"I'm sorry for giving you reason to." He held her gaze. "One of these days, we should talk. I'll answer whatever questions you have. But the most important thing you can know, is that I would never do anything to harm your daughter, or your family."

"I believe you, Rick." Mary looked over at Cathy. "I trust your judgment, Cathy, I'm sorry that I questioned it."

"Maybe if Jim had someone to protect him, and look out for him, the way you do me, none of this would have ever happened. I know everything you do, you do out of love, Mom. I'm sorry if I lost sight of that."

"What do you say we give this vacation another try?" Suzie smiled as she walked up to them. "Starting tomorrow morning, Mary is officially off for the week."

"Suzie, you can't handle everything alone."

"Oh, I won't have to, right Paul?" She grinned at him.

"Huh? Oh sure, right." Paul nodded.

"Just don't let him do the laundry." Mary laughed.

"Hey!" Paul chuckled. "Actually, that's probably for the best."

As they walked back towards Dune House, Suzie looked over her shoulder at the open water. She couldn't see the island, but she imagined that Curtis was there, putting the last rock back into place. He'd loved adventure, and though his life was short, he'd lived it fully. Even though his dishonesty had led to his death, she hoped that justice being served, would give him some peace.

The End

More Cozy Mysteries by Cindy Bell

Sage Gardens Cozy Mysteries

Birthdays Can Be Deadly

Money Can Be Deadly

Trust Can Be Deadly

Ties Can Be Deadly

Rocks Can Be Deadly

Jewelry Can Be Deadly

Numbers Can Be Deadly

Memories Can Be Deadly

Paintings Can Be Deadly

Snow Can Be Deadly

Wendy the Wedding Planner Cozy Mysteries

Matrimony, Money and Murder

Chefs, Ceremonies and Crimes

Knives and Nuptials

Mice, Marriage and Murder

Chocolate Centered Cozy Mysteries

The Sweet Smell of Murder

A Deadly Delicious Delivery

A Bitter Sweet Murder

A Treacherous Tasty Trail

Luscious Pastry at a Lethal Party

Trouble and Treats

Dune House Cozy Mysteries

Seaside Secrets

Boats and Bad Guys

Treasured History

Hidden Hideaways

Dodgy Dealings

Suspects and Surprises

Heavenly Highland Inn Cozy Mysteries

Murdering the Roses

Dead in the Daisies

Killing the Carnations

Drowning the Daffodils

Suffocating the Sunflowers

Books, Bullets and Blooms

A Deadly Serious Gardening Contest

A Bridal Bouquet and a Body

Macaron Patisserie Cozy Mysteries

Sifting for Suspects

Recipes and Revenge

Nuts about Nuts Cozy Mysteries

A Tough Case to Crack

Bekki the Beautician Cozy Mysteries

Hairspray and Homicide

A Dyed Blonde and a Dead Body

Mascara and Murder

Pageant and Poison

Conditioner and a Corpse

Mistletoe, Makeup and Murder

Hairpin, Hair Dryer and Homicide

Blush, a Bride and a Body

Shampoo and a Stiff

Cosmetics, a Cruise and a Killer

Lipstick, a Long Iron and Lifeless

Camping, Concealer and Criminals

Treated and Dyed